Awakened Blood
FOREVER BOUND SERIES
BOOK ONE

TALA MOORE

EVA KINGSLEY

Copyright © 2023 by Tala Moore & Eva Kingsley

All rights reserved.

No part of this book may be reproduced in any form or by any electronic or mechanical means, including information storage and retrieval systems, without written permission from the author, except for the use of brief quotations in a book review.

CONTENTS

	Adam	1
1.	Kiera	5
2.	Adam	11
3.	Kiera	22
4.	Adam	36
5.	Kiera	43
6.	Adam	54
7.	Kiera	65
8.	Adam	74
9.	Kiera	81
10.	Adam	88
11.	Kiera	92
12.	Adam	98
13.	Kiera	106
14.	Adam	111

Bound Blood	119
FREE Read!	121
Also by Tala Moore and Eva Kingsley	123
About the Authors	125

ADAM
1732 BC, CADELL ESTATE

Screams and the sound of thrashing and fighting echo off the stone walls of the throne room as two young women are dragged through the brocaded double doors by the Cadell legionnaires. The vampires in their golden armor and plumed red helmets aren't encumbered by the women, rather they throw them over their shoulders and toss them at the base to the stairs leading to the throne.

The great golden chair is where our father presides, myself and my four brothers flanking him. The five of us wear black plated armor with silver embellishment and black velvet capes. Each of us wears a golden circlet on our brows, while our father wears the golden crown of leaves favored by the Romanian aristocracy, his temples growing silver after millennia of life.

I glower down at the women huddled together at the base of the dais and spare a glare at my father. My brothers laugh cruelly at them, licking their lips, but it is me that my father looks upon.

"A gift...for your name day, Adam. These peasants will be your personal attendants and your source of sustenance." He stiffens. "Don't glower at me, Adam, their father sold them. I did not capture them."

I bare my fangs at my father as the women cry out and beg for mercy. "I do not drink from women who are not willing, Father, whether purchased or not. Send them back." I fold my arms over my chest, finished with the discussion, and the women look up at me with hope in their eyes. I barely look at them. They're filthy, as if they were dragged through the mud before being presented to me.

"If you will not have them, I will take them. My harem runs dry," Devion quips, taking a step towards the women.

With preternatural speed I block his path, appearing no more than a black shadow crossing the room. The women scream and begin to sob uncontrollably.

"Your *larder* runs dry because you drain every woman you take to your rooms after you've had your fill of their carnal pleasures!" The silver blue irises of the Cadell clan flare in Devion's eyes, and I know mine are doing the same. His lips peel back from his teeth as he hisses in my face and raises a hand tipped with black claws to rip me out of his way, but I toss him across the room to smash on the floor and crack the marble.

My father is laughing and the maniacal cackle grates on my nerves.

"If you will not have them, why do you protest their usage for the intended purpose?" he calls out. "Adam, my heir, you must eat. You must drain your women and find your Forever Bound. Devion does not shy from this; should he be my successor instead?" My father rests his chin on his hand, staring at me with raw intensity. I can feel Devion closing in behind me, and I prepare to send him flying.

Except Devion snarls, the same hunger filling his face as the smell of human blood permeates the room.

I turn to find the younger of the women biting her own wrist savagely, blood spilling between her teeth.

"If you're going to kill me, my Lords, just get it over with. Spare my sister, she is with child. Do not end two lives this day. I sacrifice myself to your thirst!" The young woman, so brave and passionate, raises her arm above her head and we all watch enraptured as the blood trickles down her arm freely. Her other arm is holding her trembling sister, who looks around in terror and clutches her stomach, even though she's not yet showing.

"Two for one? The richest blood I've ever had!" Devion roars as he dashes forward like a black mist. His claws dig into the pregnant sister and she screams. The younger sister throws herself at him, trying ineffectually to pull my brother off her sister. Devion just laughs and throws her aside, knocking her unconscious against a pillar.

"This won't hurt for long," Devion hisses and opens his mouth to bite the screaming sister.

I can feel my nails growing into black talons before I'm even moving. I grab Devion by the shoulder, ripping long gouges through his armor with my nails as I throw him off of the woman. His talons claw her shoulder too, leaving a mirror image of wounds on them both.

"Mine!" I hiss menacingly, using my body to shield the pregnant woman from my brother. My cloak covers her, and she clings to me for protection. "They are both... mine..." I pant, lifting the pregnant sister and cradling her against my chest. I walk over to her sister, and with one hand, throw the unconscious woman over my shoulder. With a final glare to my father, I carry my charges away from the blood thirsty throne room.

"Are you going to kill us?" the pregnant sister asks in a small voice even as she whimpers in fear.

"The blood beneath my brother's nails is the last of your

blood that will ever be spilled in my care," I growl quietly, fiercely.

I do not look at her, I look straight forward, and leave the Cadell Estate. I will take these women to my country home and leave them there. They will serve as my servants do, unbothered for the rest of their days.

CHAPTER 1
KIERA

I raise my chin, mustering up courage I don't have as the man in a blue three-piece suit introduces himself as Mateo, the human assistant to the great Lord Adam Cadell, heir to the Cadell empire. I've never been in a castle this grand before; the white marble floors are polished to a mirror-like sheen, the walls covered with Roman era paintings and memorabilia. My heels click loudly as Mateo leads me down a long corridor and the pitch black night seems to seep through to my bones like the chill in the air did.

My heart thuds in time to my footsteps, seeming to struggle in my tight chest.

I have to do this. I can't back down now. My family is depending on me...

I keep the sweet images of my grandmother, sister, and her daughter fresh in my mind, then wince as the image of the Monroe patriarch quickly follows. His hissed words slither through me.

"Fail and they die."

Who knew that my passion for history and genealogy would make me useful to them? When my father couldn't pay his debts, they decided I'd be the one to repay them as they shredded his throat.

In some ways, it's a blessing. My family and I would be dead if I didn't have a use for the Monroes.

The grand decorations and thick tapestries go by unseen as we walk down the never ending corridor, but I can see the end. Two huge, brocaded doors emblazoned with the Cadell seal; two crows in battle for a great flaming sword. The doors are identical to the Monroes throne room; except their emblem is a rose with silver thorns dripping with black vampiric blood.

My stomach flip flops painfully. Turns out vampires exist. And they have fated mates. Forever Bounds.

And it's my job to find Adam Cadell's.

The doors open before us on their own accord as we approach, and I have to hide the surprise and shock that I feel as we walk into a magnificent library with a single desk on the dais rather than a throne room. Stacks of scrolls and books are littered across the white marble floors, the arched ceilings flickering with the fire from a great burning blaze in the ornate fireplace behind the desk. It's hard to remember I'm not back in the dark ages. That beyond this castle, a modern world thrives.

Clueless to the existence of vampires.

The large office chair at the desk is facing the blaze, and as the sound of my heels echoing off the domed ceiling, the chair turns.

And my heart stutters.

The pale man in the chair is nothing short of stunning; the sensuous mouth framed by a chiseled jaw, the long dark hair are a soft contrast to the jagged scar running down the side of his face. Deep, almost brutal, it runs from eyebrow and down his cheek. He wears a white shirt, dated as it's medieval times, open at the collar with wide billowing sleeves.

Adam looks at me through thick lashes, his silver blue eyes

boring into the very core of me. Unwillingly I feel as if I've been set on fire with lust, an instant attraction that I don't need. A flash of hunger in his eyes almost made me step back and tremble. He looks like he'll devour me from the clit up... I shiver slightly, reacting to the carnal imagery my mind just conjured up.

Lord Adam Cadell, in the flesh.

The man I've been tasked with destroying.

"Keira Von Ranke, the highly recommended historian." His voice is smooth, too slick to be human as his eyes take in every curve on my body and he licks his lips. I fight the desire pooling between my legs, determined to resist the pull of his charm. They probably know how to glamor a girl.

He leans forward, practically vibrating with intensity. "And yet, no matter how skilled you are, you will fail."

I tip my chin up at him. He's as handsome as he's severe but I refuse to let him see the effect he has on me. The fear...and the unwanted draw to see if that skin feels as smooth as it looks. I step around Mateo and march up the stairs of the dais to lay my hand on his desk with a slap.

I wore a button up white silk blouse and a black pinstripe skirt over my black six-inch stilettos. I lean over the desk, knowing my cleavage is showing through the unbuttoned shirt, a silver cross necklace dangling in front of me as I lean in and glare stare for stare at the vampire. Right now, I'm glad for the cross. I didn't bank on feeling anything for this vampire.

The one I've been sent to destroy.

"I'm here to do a job, and I have never failed in my line of work. I will not fail now, and you will not intimidate me...my Lord." I raise an eyebrow at the last word, with a glance around his throne room, and sit on the edge of his desk. "I'm a specialist, and I've traced many family lines, no matter how ancient. So let's skip the formalities and get down to business."

Adam's eyebrows rise as he sits back in his chair. He folds his ankles on the desk and steeples his fingers beneath his nose with the trace of a smirk on his face. I fold my arms under my breasts and match his hard stare with my own.

I can't show him I'm afraid, even if he can hear my heart thudding out of my chest. I try not to look at him like he's looking at me...with a desperate sexual desire to rip my clothes off.

"Have you ever been bitten, Kiera?" he asks, his tongue flicking over his fangs.

I slide off the desk, one hand on my hip and one pointing directly at his nose. I have to clench my legs together to stop the unwilling throbbing growing more and more insistent inside my panties.

"This is strictly a hands—and mouth—off job, mister. Touch me even once and you jeopardize finding your own mate. How old are you? Over three hundred years? Would you rather spend another millennia alone? I didn't think so." I turn my back to him, hands on my hips.

"Disappointing..." he says, his voice dripping with hunger and masculinity, and I find myself somehow disappointed as well.

Disappointed that he would give up the urge so easily.

I glance over my shoulder as he begins sorting papers, not looking at me at all.

"Mateo has thoroughly vetted you, Miss Von Ranke. I know you are serious about your work and I know you will try your hardest to find my mate. I will not hold my breath, though," he chuckles, knowing full well he never needs to breathe.

"You'll be pleasantly surprised, as I've already done most of your background work. I have here your entire family tree..." I reach out to Mateo, who holds a large tube in his hands. Adam nods, and Mateo hands it over. Inside the tube is a large, frayed paper, as old as it is frail, and I unroll it on Adam's desk, using his books to weigh down the edges.

The key piece of information the Monroes told me is that Forever Bounds tend to be drawn to each other, life after life. That means Adam's Forever Bound is likely a woman he's met before. Probably someone he knew. She may even be in his life already.

All he has to do is drain her and if she survives, she'll be gifted a life of immortality with her fated mate.

"See here? This is the whole thing; your father, your late mother, and your four half-brothers. By far this is the sparsest family tree I've ever managed. All the Cadell men, not including your father, have never found their Forever Bound. I've scoured the records at the public archives and will begin here with your private records immediately. As old as you all are, it will be a challenge to track down every woman you have ever come in contact with, but it's a challenge I'm willing to take."

"You act as if I've hired you already, Kiera..."

I ignore the shiver my name on his lips induces. "Can you really afford *not* to hire me? To take on a less qualified genealogist? I don't think so. Let us get back to business." I point at his mother's branch of the tree, knowing full well her line was destroyed, and put a coin over her name. "We can rule out your mother's line, as she was the last living member. Did she have any friends? Any close servants? That would be the best place to start."

Adam stands, adjusting his cuffs and looking down at me seriously. "You seem very keen to take on this job, Kiera," he murmurs. "Which means you want it for reasons other than just prestige or money."

I lower my gaze, trying to appear focused on the work when the sheer size and presence of him is making my heart flutter against my will. He's handsome.

And astute.

"My family is overseas, having traveled to America after the last wars. I want to build a life for us there, in Europe. Or homeland." I raise my chin, letting him see the truth in my words.

I need to take my family far away, as far from the Cadells and Monroes as possible.

I settle my hands on my hips as I hold his gaze. "I'm the only one who can do this, and I'm the best you could ever ask for."

Adam lets his gaze drift from my face to my breasts, and he lingers on my exposed legs below the skirt. The way he's looking at me has nothing to do with his Forever Bound or finding her, and everything to do with his cock. He scowls and looks away from me, but I can see he's still staring down my blouse from the corner of his eye. His fists clench and unclench as he struggles with his own internal desires. Is he feeling the same pull to me as I feel for him?

Doubtful, he's probably just hungry.

He seems to reach a decision as he turns his gaze back to me, those silver blue eyes hard once more. "Then it's final. These are my personal records for the entire Cadell line. Get to work." He walks around his desk, pausing a hair's breadth away from me, and speaks directly into my ear. "Do not disappoint me, human," he threatens, before turning on a heel and storming out of the throne room.

As soon as the door slams behind Mateo and Adam, I brace my shaking arms on the desk. I have too much on the line to disappoint him, but the heat curling between my legs says it's going to be more than my life hanging in the balance.

If I'm not careful, my heart will be too.

CHAPTER 2
ADAM

"Get to the castle swiftly, Mateo. There's much work to do today."

Mateo nods at me as he opens the door to the limousine and I slip inside. As we leave my private penthouse, I find I still cannot get Kiera off my mind. I think back to the way she sways as she walks, the warm honey and sugar perfume she wears. When she came into my presence her scent overwhelmed me, and with every haughty toss of her wavy brown hair her scent encompassed me even more.

Mateo clears his throat from the front of the limo and I snap out of my reverie. I do not have time to be distracted by a human! She's nothing but a tool to find my Forever Bound.

The search that I already know will be fruitless, but must endure so my father does not discover the truth.

Snarling at the twisted position fate has put me in, I sit forward and pour myself a glass of warm blood from the heated compartment in the limo. I raise the crystal goblet to my lips and Kiera's green eyes flash in my memory as they did when she saw me eyeing her jugular vein...then the much more entertaining veins on her inner thighs. When Mateo stops the limo in front of the castle, the blood spills over my hand, once again snapping me back to attention.

"Stop more carefully next time, Mateo. You may be my right-hand man, but right now my right hand is covered with blood. If I wanted to get blood on the cuffs of my shirt, I'd eat straight from a human." I flick the blood off my hand as Mateo laughs and opens my door, handing me a wet wipe.

"I drive the same every day, my Lord. It seems your mind is lingering somewhere else... somewhere you could get real messy." He winks at me and I scowl.

Mateo's been my best friend for years, only he can talk to me like this and live. I wipe the blood from my hand and glare at the stain on my white shirt and suit jacket sleeve. I smirk. Maybe seeing blood on me will shake the woman when she arrives. She could use a dose of fear with all that fire in her soul.

We walk through the castle as servants and employees scurry around and out of my way. Each of them carries papers or scrolls, and all look harried and exhausted. I exchange a glance with Mateo and he shrugs, opening the door to my office.

There, sitting on my desk and absorbed in studying, is Keira. Today she wears black slacks and a white blouse only halfway buttoned over a red, low-cut camisole. I stop in my tracks, watching her kick her stiletto heel as she bites the end of a pencil. All around her my people are scouring the histories, and as she looks up as they scatter.

She has them all working for her...

"How nice to see you here. Did you get your rest?" Those green eyes lock with mine and the smirk on her red lips makes my cock stiffen on command.

"How long have you been here, Kiera?" I ask her sternly, folding my arms over my chest and nodding to my servants as if to ask her how she managed to make the whole castle do her bidding.

Kiera slides off my desk and walks to me, her hips swaying and I have to look away. I cannot look at her walk like that and remain sound of mind. I roll my eyes, trying to appear nonchalant, but when she stands in front of me, her warm honey scent fills my nostrils and my eyes lock on hers as if magnetized.

"I never left, my Lord. Worked all through the night. This is going to take longer than I imagined. Time that you and I don't have." She hands me a scroll with my father's crest on it. I scowl when I register the seal has been broken. "This arrived not long ago. Your father's summoned you to the seaside enclave. Apparently, you and your brothers must come immediately."

I scowl at Mateo, who shrugs and walks away as I take the scroll from Kiera and her delicate fingers brush mine. I'm momentarily distracted by her elegant fingers and long red nails as a rush of desire runs up my arm like lightning.

"There's no time to waste worrying about your correspondence being exposed to me," Kiera continues, arching a brow. "As your historian, I must record all information, both present and past. Had that letter stated a Forever Bound was located for you or your brothers, it would have been vital to my research."

She flips her thick hair off one shoulder and I resist the urge to inhale her scent. I try to read the summons, but my eyes are glued to the curve of her neck, the sweat that glistens on her soft skin.

I resist the desire to wipe it away with my finger and taste the salty sweetness of her efforts in my family home.

She shuffles through the stacks of papers in her arms. "Before you leave, my Lord, I must make a record of every woman you've crossed paths with so I can trace their lineage and cross check living women in your life today."

I narrow my eyes at her. "No, the summons says immediately, I've kept enough journals for you to find the information yourself."

She glares up at me and grabs the sleeve of my jacket, pulling me towards a floor to ceiling bookcase with black bound books marked only with the year they were written.

"Adam, you have hundreds upon hundreds of journals. I'm not superhuman. In the time we have, I can't possibly read every journal you've ever written. I'm the best at my job, but in the end I'm one human woman and I actually need to sleep, unlike your kind."

My lips twitch against my will as she taps her toes at me. She's much smaller than me, a good two feet shorter, yet full of fire and sass. I look down at the silver cross resting in her cleavage and realize I can see the flesh of her stomach from this position standing above her.

Maybe I have time after all.

I roll my neck, letting the stiff muscles crack as I stretch. I walk over to a sitting area and take a seat on a long couch and cross my legs. With a wave of my hand, I offer her a seat next to me and she hurries to my desk to grab a notebook and her pencil. I watch the way her ass bounces as she climbs the stairs and I imagine that ass bouncing on my face as I taste her at her core.

"Adam?"

She interrupts my fantasy, and I gaze at her. She's sitting on the cushion right next to me, pencil poised on the paper and a gleam of eagerness in her eyes. I watch her body pucker with goosebumps as I lick my lips and take in how sexy she looks sitting with me on the couch where I've bedded many women.

"I'm a very private man, Kiera. I will give you only names and years." I finger the scar that cuts through my face. I will not divulge personal information if she'll not read it for herself. If she wants details, she can find them.

Kiera rolls her eyes and slams the notebook down on her lap. "How about you just go out at night and drain every woman you cross? One of them is bound to survive, and it would be quicker than you wasting my time." She arches a brow, challenging me.

phoShe clears her throat and puts her hands on my suit jacket, fire forming in her eyes as her attitude changes from fear to anger. "And when you drain me and I die on this couch, you lose a damn good genealogist and you're back to square one." She pushes me forcefully, and though her feeble strength could never move me, I sit back in my seat and straighten my jacket. I watch her legs tremble as she lays there, trying to catch her breath. No, I will not drain her. The thought of her dying in my arms is not a picture I want to see.

With my reverie of sex and blood broken, I speak as she sits up and straightens her clothes. "Where would you like to start?" I loosen the tie around my throat and take off my suit jacket.

Kiera is back to fire and brimstone, her back straight as the pillars in this throne room. "Let's start with the obvious. How often do you start a new life? To keep the humans in the dark about your true origins?" She bites her bottom lip.

Fire and brimstone...and desire. I can smell it coming off of her.

"Every hundred years," I tell her as I lean forward, watching her scribble down notes and trying to get a deeper scent of her sexual desires.

"Surely not!" Her head whips up and she realizes how close I am. I watch her throat bob as she swallows and imagine her swallowing my seed...

"I'm a reclusive person," I say with a shrug and a cold smile as she scoots away ever so slightly. "And it's not like many humans look upon my face and pay any kind of attention rather than irrational fear." I put my arm behind her on the couch and she inhales sharply.

I wonder how I smell to her...

"So we go...what? A hundred years at a time?" Nervously she fiddles with her cross necklace, and I reach toward her and take it from her hands.

"You do know that while silver can kill a vampire, it has to puncture our hearts to do so. Wearing silver does not affect me," I whisper, waving my servants out of the room. I slide my pinkie on her breast as I hold the necklace and pull her closer. "It only draws further attention to your breasts."

"I...didn't know that."

She's lying. I can hear her heart skip a beat. She puts her hands on my chest to shove me away but she doesn't push. Her fingers trace the outline of my heavily muscled chest and she bites her lip. With a broken snarl, I rip the necklace off her neck and throw it, using my other hand to take a handful of hair at the nape of her neck.

And kiss those lush, parted lips.

Keira gasps as if she was intending on denying this, but she instantly melts on a moan. I slip my tongue in her mouth to find she tastes like peppermint and coffee. She moans again and I'm instantly rock hard. I've kissed many women, but never has it felt like this. Fire courses through my veins as I wrap my arm around her waist and her arms go around my neck in halting movements. She's fighting her urges, but the scent of her passion grows with every passing second.

My kisses go from forceful to needy. She stands on her knees on the couch and crawls over my lap, never once breaking the kiss as she straddles my hips. The moment she feels my hard cock against her pants, she moans, throwing her head back and rocking her core against it. She glares down at me. She didn't want this; but she cannot stop herself just as much as I cannot.

I raise my hands to her shirt, my fingers growing black talons as I lose control. Her pants are wet through, the proof of her pleasure soaking my slacks, making the imprint of my cock more and more apparent. I rip her shirt open, undershirt, bra and all, exposing two perfect breasts. She gasps and tries to cover herself, but I pin her arms behind her back with one hand and gaze at her in awe.

Her nipples are so pale they seem to have no areola at all. I've never seen a pair of breasts so unique, so perfect. I flick a claw over a hard nub and she gasps, beginning to rock on my cock again as I lower my head to taste her pink flesh and suck on her pert nipple.

Mateo clears his throat and I clutch Kiera to my chest, blocking her bare breasts from my man's view. She is mine. No other man will look upon her sweet flesh but me. I turn my head and hiss at him, rocking my hard cock into her pants even as she struggles to make me let her go.

"My Lord, a helicopter has landed. Apparently, your father and brothers tire of waiting for you. They are here now."

I growl menacingly and bury my face in Kiera's brown curls, nuzzling her neck before running my fangs down her throat. She shivers and tries to stifle a moan. I slip my hand down into her pants and between the folds of her sex, circling her clit once before pulling my hand out and sucking the taste of her off my finger.

I lock eyes with her as I lick a long talon, savoring the taste of her on my tongue. I swear she almost comes watching me lick her juices off me, and I'm delighted to find she does, in fact, taste like warm honey. I kiss her again, making her taste herself on my lips when Mateo clears his throat again, louder and more insistent.

I growl and set Keira on the couch, taking off my shirt and handing it to her. She looks up at me in awe. My chest is thickly muscled and covered with a peppering of curly black hair. Nearly every inch of my body is covered in scars from silver blades in battles past. She runs a hand down the middle of my chest and grabs a hold of my belt forcefully. Her face is the very picture of lust, and I wish nothing more in that moment to have that red mouth wrap around my cock.

"Take her away, hide her in my private rooms. Inform all female servants to make themselves scarce." I force her hand off my pants and she actually snarls at me. I chuckle, leaving the room in only my slacks to meet my family in the foyer.

My father, still wearing the lavish velvet robes of kings in the medieval era, stands impatiently in the foyer, his hands resting on a tall golden cane that we all know has a silver blade inside. My brothers fan out around him as I approach, each in a modern suit, each with their hair cut short and quaffed to the latest styles of the century.

"Zarius, my dear father." I hug him soundly and nod to my brothers; Brec, Corbett, Devion, and the youngest; Ever. "It is good to see you, blood of my blood."

They all nod in return, no one speaking.

My father steps forward. "Adam, you ignored my summons. I expected you immediately. Your younger brothers did not disappoint me. You? I have to track you down at my ancestral home. How many times in your long life have I summoned you in such a way? Never. You should have come." Zarius shrugs my hands off his shoulder and walks past me, my brothers following him single file and each giving me their own brand of "You're a fuck up" glares.

I clench my fist and flex my muscles as they walk away from me, trying to keep my composure. My father is headed for his study and he doesn't plan to wait for an invitation.

"I have spent my time in Europe," my father announces from his throne inside the massive room lined with leather bound books.

We stand in a semi-circle around him, knowing exactly what he's been doing. My father found his Forever Bound, my mother, only to lose her when she was assassinated. His life-long quest to find her again has left a trail of dead women behind him, including my brother's mothers. I stopped looking at them centuries ago. It's easier not knowing who they are.

"It was there that I learned troubling news. The Monroes, our sworn enemy, want Sorin City."

A growl ripples through my brothers. Sorin City is Cadell land and the Monroes know it.

My father nods, acknowledging the fury his words spark. "I've had word they intend to target your Forever Bounds. Without them, we cannot have daughters and they know that." He pauses, looking at all of us gravely, and a chill runs down my spine as my brothers hiss and roar.

"Now, more than ever, it is imperative that you find and protect your Forever Bound. We must strengthen our lineage. If you do not, they will attack and steal our city."

"And if we cannot find them? Like you have never been able to?" Brec snaps. "Do we just have children with whomever as you did?"

Ever looks between all his brothers, fear in his eyes. He's only a century old and hasn't even thought about a mate.

"Does your chest feel empty? Does your soul feel scattered to the seven seas?" Corbett faces our brother, his hand gripping his collar and shouting into his face. "If you feel these things, then your mate is out there. It is that yearning that drove our father. Finding our Forever Bound will save those women you profess to protect."

Brec rips Corbett's fist off him and glares at me.

And yet I find myself without words. I may be Zarius's eldest, the son of a Forever Bound, but I carry a secret none of them know.

I already know who my Forever Bound is...

"Enough!" Zarius roars. "Fighting amongst ourselves is a sign of weakness! Get out there! Find your mates! Now!" My father stands, pulling his sword from his cane and pointing it at each of us. "Find your mates, or discover the edge of my sword."

"My Lord?" I turn my head in a snap to see Mateo standing in the doorway. He knows to never interrupt me when I'm with my family unless it's an emergency. My mind immediately goes to Kiera, but she's there behind him with a determined look on her face. There's only one other woman who would have such a profound effect on Mateo for him to risk his life. I'm there in the shadow of a flash, my hands on his shoulders.

"Where is she? Where is Marianna?"

Mateo's sister, the only reason he'd risk death for is her.

"Club Black," he whispers.

"I'm coming, and you can't stop me." Kiera stands her ground, and stares down my family without a hint of fear. "If I'm going to find your mate, Adam, I must know all the women you are affiliated with. This is the best place to start."

I grab her elbow and pull her away from the room as my brothers begin to argue over how I don't have the right to hire a beautiful woman to find my mate when Kiera could be their own mate. Mateo hands me a new shirt as we rush to the garages.

We approach my personal car, a custom Tesla. I slide into the driver's seat and take the wheel, glaring menacingly at

Mateo as he tries to take the passenger seat. He nods and opens the door for Kiera, and as she slips into the seat, I put a possessive hand on her thigh.

The moment Mateo is sitting, I punch the gas and peel out of the garage.

CHAPTER 3
KIERA

I can feel the bass pounding in my bones. Strobe lights and glitter confetti rain from the ceiling as Mateo leads us through a crowd of gyrating humans. Nervously, I glance from the scantily clad women to the vampire behind me; can he be trusted here? Much to my surprise, Adam's eyes are on me as if I'm the only woman in the world. He has a fist to his chest and a look of worry on his face. We lock eyes and he grabs my hand to pull me close. I instinctively tuck myself under his arm and wrap my own around his back.

I realize at this moment that I've never felt more safe with any other man, and this is the only man who I've ever let hold me like this who wants to suck my blood. As people push by us, Adam shields me from being jostled, putting himself between me and the raucous crowd and my cheeks flush. I clutch his shirt as he twists and turns in the crowd. I've never felt like a damsel in distress in my life, but something about Adam makes me feel as if I don't have to act so strong anymore.

Mateo stops in front of a women's bathroom door. "She's in here…" he says, but doesn't open it.

I'm only human, but even I can smell the sharpness of blood

through the closed door. Adam's nostrils flare and even though his mouth is shut, I can see his canines elongate behind his lips.

"I'll go in," I volunteer. "It's usually frowned upon for a man to enter a woman's toilet." I smile slightly at Mateo and push open the door, but the moment Adam sees the woman on the floor, the things that may be frowned upon no longer matter.

Surrounding the woman are several inebriated women in stages of undress. They're all watching her worried, but none move to help. I push them aside and kneel in front of a deathly pale Latina woman. She's halfway inside of a toilet cubicle, her legs sticking out into the main bathroom. She cradles her hands to her chest and I can see long slices in her skin from wrist to elbow.

"She started screaming and then broke a mirror!" a drunk bystander yells over the music. "She used the glass to cut herself!"

Adam pushes by me and checks the girl's pulse. She's unconscious, but alive. We turn to Mateo, who has tears streaming down his face, a phone to his ear, calling his parents. I expected him to be more of a wreck, but he only nods to Adam and turns away. Mateo pushes every woman out of the bathroom with promises that his sister will be just fine and there's no need to call an ambulance.

I turn back to Adam just in time to watch him lick the woman's wound, starting at her inner elbow all the way up to her wrist. I reach out to stop him, absolutely appalled that he would take advantage of Mateo's sister at a time like this, but as Adam gently lowers one arm and grabs the other, I notice that the grievous wounds are mending themselves at lightning speed. I sit back on my heels in shock. Adam is taking no pleasure from the taste of her blood in a time of weakness; he's healing her.

Slowly, Mateo's sister begins to stir awake and Adam gently

helps her to her feet and scoops her up into his arms. "Marianna..." Adam whispers, and her eyes fly open. The air around us goes thick as Adam locks eyes with her, his voice growing low and commanding. "Marianna, you will never hurt yourself again. If you feel the need to self-harm, you will come directly to Mateo or I."

Marianna looks at him as if in a daze, and nods. The tension in the room eases and I realize I just witnessed vampire compulsion in action.

I stare in awe at the gentle way Adam cradles Marianna, and I realize that there's a tender, caring man behind the visage of a heartless monster. Something in my chest tightens as I watch him set Marianna down to sit on the counter. With every passing moment in Adam's presence, I feel more and more drawn to him.

Even if it can never be.

I watch him push the hair out of Marianna's face as she slowly comes to, and dread blooms in my chest. I could very well be looking at his Forever Bound. Seeing his hands on her raises a temper in me I never knew I had, and before I can register it as jealousy, I speak.

"Alright, she's ok, no more men in the women's bathroom!" I grab Adam by the collar and pull him back towards the door.

I push him into Mateo and shove them both out of the bathroom and lock the door behind them. With a humph, I straighten my clothes, flip my curls over my shoulder, and turn to face Marianna.

Marianna, who is very likely the mate of the man I almost boned on a couch in a library an hour ago.

"W-what happened?" Marianna asks me. "Where am I?" She rubs her eyes as she starts to cry. The poor girl is drunk and doesn't remember a thing.

"Marianna, right? Hon, you passed out on the dance floor.

Little too much to drink, eh?" I lie as I wet a paper towel and start to wipe the tears from her face and clean the sweat and glitter away from her eyes. "Luckily, someone found your phone and your emergency contact was right on the front of the screen. That's the smartest thing I've ever seen. Mateo brought us here, but it's just you and me now, so no need to feel embarrassed."

Marianna blushes hard, hiding her face in shame. "I'm so sorry to trouble you...?" She looks up at me questioningly.

"Kiera, I'm Kiera," I answer.

"Kiera, I'm so sorry. I tend to faint even when I'm not drinking." She chuckles depreciatively, rubbing her forearms. "At least I don't cut anymore, right?"

"Right, that would have been very bad to walk in on for sure. Are you feeling better now?" I put my hands on her shoulders, trying to steady her as her body weaves on the counter of its own accord.

She looks up at me and smiles. "Gosh, you're pretty. Are you Mateo's girlfriend? I've always wanted a sister." Marianna hiccups and I swear I can feel overwhelming jealousy pouring through the bathroom door from where Mateo and Adam are waiting. "Yeah, I'm fine. Weird things just trigger me sometimes. I'm flooded with an overwhelming sadness that I can't handle. Like, there's no reason for me to be sad, ya know? I'm having a great night! But the pain, Kiera, just comes out of nowhere. I'll see the shadow of a man in the corner of my eye, but there's no one there. And then the sadness hits, weighing me down like there are bricks tied to my ankles and I'm sinking in the water..."

I pull her in for a hug and she starts sobbing wildly on my shoulder.

"I just don't know what to do anymore!" Marianna hiccups loudly. "I can't stop it! I can't get too drunk not to feel it, I can't get too high not to care. I'm running from some unseen fear and I feel like I'm losing my mind!"

I stroke her hair and make gentle shushing noises as she clings to me and cries. "It's gonna be alright, Mari, okay?" I pull back, smiling into her tear-streaked face. "Hey, why don't we go to lunch sometime? I can already sense we're going to be great friends."

Marianna wipes away her tears as she nods. "That sounds like a lot of fun." She laughs, and I hug her again, finding I was telling the truth. I feel close to her, as if I've known her my whole life.

Yet, even as I think it, a dark feeling blooms in my stomach. I also need to investigate Marianna's connection to Adam. She could be his Forever Bound, and even if that makes me feel irrational jealousy, I have to do what's right and find out for sure.

As we exit the bathroom, I can't meet her gaze, let alone Adam's. I imagine myself killing her, as per the Monroes command.

And I feel sick to my stomach.

After Adam drives Mateo and Marianna to their family home, he takes us back to the castle. I notice as we pull into the garage that the helicopter is gone, and so are the rest of the Cadell brothers. I follow Adam blindly through the house, my mind already trying to wrap itself around the gentlest way to kill Marianna if she's his Forever Bound.

I finally snap back to reality when Adam takes off his shirt right in front of me, slowly. Deliberately.

I watch every button come down as if in a trance.

Only then do I realize we're in a bedchamber.

Adam's looking at me with an eyebrow cocked as he drops the shirt on the floor and I see Marianna's blood on the sleeves.

"Oh, you got blood on you. That's why you're taking your shirt off!" I say dumbly.

Adam chuckles and starts walking towards me. He's seductive beyond reason with the stealthy way he walks, and I feel my stomach clench as the familiar burn of passion rips through me. Flustered, I step back as he prowls closer and closer, until I feel my back hit the wall. Adam leans over me, placing his hand on the wall, and I stare in awe at the scars and curls of hair on his chest, nearly losing myself in how badly I want to touch him.

Grasping at my last thread of coherent thought, I let a question bubble up my throat. "Who is Marianna to you?" I swallow as his face moves closer, his mouth a hair's breadth from my lips. I have to focus. I cannot be feeling this way about my enemy. I have to turn myself off, and fucking now!

"Mateo's family has worked for my family for years. I owe it to protect them, as they have served me for millennia." He twirls a finger in my hair before he tucks the strand behind my ear. "Now where did we leave off..."

"Surely her past lives are entangled with yours. You could have just healed your own Forever Bound tonight."

Adam takes a deep breath, one that he doesn't need, and steps back. He looks annoyed, but I thank the stars for the distance. "She's not the one," he says, his face going hard as he walks to a table with a steaming pitcher on it.

"Well...how do you know?" I ask, pushing myself off the wall and following him, trying to be business-like.

"I just know!" he says sharply as he pours warm fresh blood into a crystal goblet. "I'd feel it." He sets the pitcher down and takes a drink.

I watch a drop of blood slip past his lips and down his jaw

and find that I am not the least bit appalled that he's drinking human blood right in front of me. I have to fight the urge to lick it off his face, deeply ashamed of even the thought itself.

"The 'I'd feel it' system hasn't seemed to work for you so far, has it? Maybe I'm right and *you're* wrong." I take a step back as he turns his severe gray eyes to me and growls.

"It. Is. Not. Marianna...she doesn't fit." His voice is hard and threatening as he glares down at me and I have to reign in my flight or fight response and stand perfectly still, pretending to be unfazed.

"She doesn't fit? What does that mean?" I counter, my hands on my hips as I face him glare for glare.

"That's right, she would never fit. She could never grasp the concept of what it would be like to be my Forever Bound. She'd be miserable." He watches me from the corner of his eye as he takes another sip, then goes to sit on the bed as he removes his shoes.

"And what, exactly, does being your Forever Bound entail... my Lord?" I say the last with thick sarcasm and he looks up at me through his brows and smirks.

"I don't like company. I prefer to be alone most of the time. I work ungodly hours, long hard hours, and that won't change for any woman. She would be here only to continue the family line."

"Lucky girl," I say dryly, and his eyes flash in anger.

"My Forever Bound will never have to worry about anything ever again. She'll want for nothing, and her every whim will be done as she sees fit. The immortality in itself is worth the price."

"Right, and she'll be shackled to a cold-hearted man who doesn't love her and only comes to her to fill her with babies. What a dream come true." I cock my head to the side as he stands in anger, his fists clenching at his sides. "Could your

Forever Bound be a dog? That life would be heaven for a labrador."

I brace myself for his fury to unleash, even drawing in a bracing breath, but Adam throws his head back...and laughs.

The sound bounces around the large bedchamber, filling the air, filling me. I have to stop my hand from moving up to my chest and pressing down, trying to keep the wondrous feeling there longer.

Adam sits back down on the bed, chuckles still rippling through him, and lays back on the bedspread. "A dog, huh? I've heard of a golden retriever boyfriend but that's a new one for me." He rolls over on his side and props his head up with his hand.

As his laughter dies, he notices that I'm staring at him.

The way he looks there on the bed is intoxicating. His six-pack tightens with every peal of laughter and I remember just how badly I want to touch him. I remember earlier when I straddled his cock and rubbed on him like a wild animal. I remember the copper and smoke taste on his tongue. When I look back to his eyes, I see he's staring at me with the same intensity I'm feeling.

Adam licks his lips and sits up, reaching out and grabbing my hips and pulling me close. I make no attempt to stop him, my mind overwhelmed with a haze of lust and desire. I put my hands on his chest, finally feeling those power muscles with my fingertips. I trace a line down a gruesome scar and my other hand slips behind his neck and into the mass of midnight black curls that trail down.

I lose all control of myself as I climb on his lap again. It's as if I'm no longer controlling my body, as if his cock is calling me to bury it inside me. Adam wraps strong arms around me and holds me close, each of us staring into each other's eyes with insatiable hunger but neither of us making the first move.

He pulls me closer as he scoots back on the bed and he lays down underneath me, taking my hands and running my fingers down his chest as if giving me permission to explore every inch of him. I stare at him, his long black hair fanned out underneath his head, his pale skin in contrast to the black velvet comforter. I marvel at how soft his hair is as I run my hands down the trail that leads to the pinnacle of my desire.

Adam bucks underneath me, running the insanely hard length of him between my legs and I moan. As if the moan was the last barrier holding him back, he grabs me and flips me underneath him. With one hand on the headboard behind us and one elbow on the bed, he grinds against my pants. His eyes are locked on mine as I wrap my legs around his waist and moan.

Never in my life has dry humping felt this absolutely amazing. As we grind together I unbutton my shirt, the shirt he took off his own back for me, and spread it open just enough for him to watch my breasts jiggle and sway with the motion between us.

I look up at him, knowing exactly what I just did, and entangle my hands in his hair at the back of his neck and try to pull him down to me.

"You dirty little vixen..." he growls, sitting up on his knees and forcing me to let go of him. "That's not where I want to kiss you this time." He grabs my hands and acts like he's going to have me undo his pants, but with a flick of a wrist, his belt is off and locked around my wrists.

"You took control last time, vixen. This time, you're mine to torture." He pulls my hands above my head and ties my wrists and the belt to the cast iron bed frame.

I can't help it, I start to panic. Is he going to drain me? Is he going to kill me right here and now? But before I can protest, he rips my pants off and throws them across the room, his hand cupping the tender flesh between my thighs forcefully.

"This..." He sighs and looks down at my body, my waxed mound, the wetness already dripping out of me. "This is where I want to kiss you."

The fear is gone as fast as it came, and the whore in me reacts. I push myself against his hand, spreading my legs and moaning, my eyes shut tight. I'm no virgin, far from it, but something about his flesh on mine is driving me crazy. I pull against the belt tying me down. I want to grab him, ride him, fuck him until he can't come anymore.

"Shh...quiet now...you better behave for me or I won't let you come..."

I look up at him, desperate. He's oozing sex appeal and power, and as he lowers himself to his knees at the end of the bed, I watch every muscle in his body move and flex. He looks like a lion, preparing to pounce on his kill. His hands grip my thighs, running slowly and firmly down to my knees, and my legs start to shake in anticipation.

Adam nibbles on the flesh next to my knee and I moan loudly, his canines running sharp lines as he grazes me on the way to my apex. He nips and sucks, kissing here and biting there, sharing the attention to both of my thighs.

But he doesn't touch me where I need him to.

I attempt to buck, to scoot closer to his mouth, but he holds me down by wrapping his arm around my legs and pinning my hips to the bed.

"This is not fair..." I gasp, our eyes locked as he blows a stream of cold air on the lips he said he wants to kiss so badly.

I almost come right then and there. I arch my back and almost scream, biting the pillow under my head in frustration.

"You're used to having control, aren't you, Kiera? You've never been with a man who could overpower you, have you?"

His kisses grow ever closer to where I need him to lick and suck, but he goes slower and slower, licking the crevice between my thigh and my labia, gripping the opposite thigh as he grins evilly from between my legs.

I scream in frustration, and he runs a thumb over the very top of my mound, stopping at my lips and pulling the flesh up. I can feel it as my clit is exposed. He stretches me open with a finger and thumb, gazing at the very core of me, letting out a gentle laugh as I squirm, breathing purposely on the tender flesh.

"Is this what you want?" His thumb flicks my clit, barely touching it, and a flood of fluid escapes me. Not quite an orgasm, but it felt almost as good as any orgasm I've ever had.

"Yes! Please.. Adam, please..." I whine, bucking and grinding my hips helplessly in his grip.

"I like it when you beg, Kiera..." he says, his voice thick with passion, and he flicks my clit with his tongue once. I scream, and he flicks it again. I moan, bucking wildly and begging for more with every undulation of my body. I've lost all sense of self, there is only need. I need him to suck it, lick it, bite it, and then I need to ride him like my life depends on it.

"Good girl..." he groans and lowers his face to suck me into his mouth completely.

I'm lost in the moans and screams. He holds onto me like I'm a wild animal, and maybe I am. I buck and ride his face, losing myself in every pass of his tongue, in every stroke of his fangs on my tender flesh. I find myself completely absorbed with the thought of him biting down and gorging on my blood as he sucks my clit, and I don't have enough presence of mind to be disgusted with myself for the thought.

Enemy...he's the enemy...but no enemy in the history of the world could suck a pussy like this.

I feel myself getting closer and closer to having the hardest and most wild orgasm of my life when Adam pulls away, sitting up on his knees and grinning at me. My juices have coated his mouth and chin, making his skin glisten.

"Don't stop, oh my god I was almost there!" I scream and try to kick him, but he grabs my foot and nips my ankle.

"You're going to come, don't you worry, but the first time I make you come I want to be deep inside you."

I gasp. No one has ever talked to me like this. As I watch him, I'm absolutely feral. He puts my leg over his shoulder and unbuttons his pants. Too slow... He's moving too slow...

I watch him rise out of his pants as if it's the first cock I've ever seen. He's absolutely massive, so thick I'm not sure my hand could fit around him. I arch my back and moan as he kisses my ankle and rubs the head of his glorious cock up and down the slit at my core. He's enjoying this too much, I realize, as he pushes just the head inside me and pulls out, rubbing up and down again. This gives me an idea, tortured as I am, to get fucked and get fucked now.

"If you keep teasing me like this..." I bite out between moans, "I'm gonna come all over your bed and not all over the fucking cock!" I glare up at him and he grins down at me like a cat who's caught a canary. Right as I'm about to scream in frustration, he plunges into me hard and fast, and stops.

I scream with pleasure, moaning as wave after wave of chills flow through my body, relishing in every moment as I feel myself stretch around that massive length. I open my eyes to find Adam completely enraptured. His face is the picture of surprise and lust, and in that moment he loses control. He grabs my legs and throws them around his hips, laying over me and fucking me like a wild animal.

It's the hardest fuck I've ever had, and I cling to him for dear life as he pounds into me over and over, his body crushing mine as he buries his face in my hair and bites down, hair and pillow in his mouth. He grunts and groans wildly, having lost all control, and I'm no longer thinking about anything at all but how full I am with him inside me. Every time he pushes in our hips meet, and I know every inch of him is inside. I've never felt this, so completely filled, so utterly pleasured.

I want to kiss him, grab him by his hair and force his mouth to mine, but I can't. He growls low in his throat, his lips brushing my ear, and I unravel. I lift my hips off the bed, fucking him just as hard as he's fucking me as I come. I cry out, whimper, whine and I don't even have a moment to feel ashamed, to worry about the velvet comforter beneath us as I come again.

Adam roars with pleasure, lifting his head up and watching my face as my body clenches his cock so hard he can barely pull in and out. I lock eyes with him as I come a third time, the bed beneath us entirely soaked with my pleasure. Adam grabs my chin, renewing his efforts inside me as the orgasm begins to fade.

He kisses me for the first time tonight, his mouth hard and soft at the same time, his tongue like molten lava as it brushes mine. I trap his tongue with my lips, sucking on it like I hope to suck his cock soon, and with a powerful thrust and a groan he loses himself inside me.

Wave after wave of hot seed fills me. I can feel it seeping out of my body, dripping down my legs. I release suction on his tongue and kiss him gently, tenderly, and he begins thrusting again even as his seed is still coming. Finally, he thrusts in harder than ever and holds it there. Our eyes lock and we come together one final time. Moaning into each other's mouths as we ride the final waves of passion before he collapses on top of me and I feel his cock go soft inside.

With one hand tucked behind my head, he kisses me gently again and takes his belt off my wrists with his other. I lower my hands and wrap my arms around his neck, kissing him passionately and trailing small circles with my nails on his hard back. He shivers with pleasure and rolls over, pulling me into the crook of his shoulder and releasing that beautiful cock from my body. I smile and nuzzle closer, rubbing my face against his chest and wrapping my arm over his waist. He kisses the top of my head and I snap back to reality.

With a jolt I hop off the bed before he can stop me, grabbing my pants from where he threw them on the floor and finding they're not destroyed. I can't, however, find my panties. I pull my slacks on regardless and start buttoning up the shirt that never made it all the way off.

"What are you doing?" Adam asks me from bed. He's stroking his cock and I can see he's getting hard again already.

I stifle a moan as I put my shoes back on. "I'm going back to work, I have a job to do, you know?" I twist my long hair into a knot and walk towards the door, my hand resting on the doorknob as I turn and say over my shoulder. "I'm going to go research Marianna's past lives. Regardless of how you feel, it's my job to prove she is or isn't your Forever Bound."

Leaving no time for him to retort, I exit the room and slam the door.

Outside, I lean on the door, one hand on the knob and the other on my throat. "What did I just do?" I whisper out loud.

Something I can never do again, I swear to myself as I quickly make my way to the throne room.

CHAPTER 4
ADAM

I sit at my desk and shuffle through my journals. I'm trying to find relevant history that Kiera can study when I'm not around. When I'm with that woman I simply cannot think clearly, and after last night? I see only her pink body as it rolls through the waves of passion I gave her. I hear only the little whimpers and screams as I touch her, kiss her...fuck her... My cock grows hard as I think of her beneath me every night for all of our nights.

As I rub my burgeoning length through my slacks, I see a post it note on my desk lamp. It's her writing, her perfect cursive scrawl. It's almost as beautiful as calligraphy and as I read it, I freeze, my cock going limp as fast as it rose.

First hundred years of Adam's life marked clear. Start the 1700s journals tomorrow, his Forever Bound has to be there.

My Forever Bound, not Kiera. Kiera's own writing reminds me that she's not mine, no matter how my heart calls for her.

She cannot be and this search of hers will be fruitless. I know this as much as I know Marianna is not my fated mate.

Frustrated, I stand and walk over to the grand fireplace behind my desk. I brace both hands on the mantel and glare into the roaring fire, and in the flames I see Kiera on her knees... begging for my cock in her mouth. I almost spill my seed in my pants when I hear the door open behind me.

"Have you seen the news?" Mateo asks, taking the stairs of the dais two at a time.

I drop one arm and look at him through a shield of my hair, making a solemn promise to myself that if he interrupts my fantasies one more time, I'll lock him in the dungeons. I won't do it, but the thought makes me feel a little better. I'm so hard it hurts and I wonder where Kiera is now, if I can get the vixen to fulfill the fantasy of her mouth on my cock. Mateo hands me his phone, opens a news video, and I press play.

"—Club Black is up in flames," the reporter continues. "We believe the fire began shortly before dawn. Many people could be heard inside, screaming for help, but the first responders couldn't get into the building. Now as they dig through the ashes, they take a body count, and not, unfortunately, a count of survivors. A harrowing day for Sorin City."

With a growl, I throw Mateo's phone into the fire. He doesn't flinch, just opens a filing cabinet full of brand new phones that sits by the fire. He perches on the corner of my desk and opens the box, as he does at least twice a month. The coals of the fire are littered with the skeletons of technology.

"This is the Monroes work!" I roar, my fingers lengthening into talons and my eyes going dark. I feel strength ripple through me and my muscles bunch and flex, almost splitting my shirt with the tension. Mateo hands me a goblet of blood to calm me, but I slap it out of his hand and the crystal glass shatters on the mantle of the fireplace. "They saw me there, saw me care about you and sister, and because I care they destroyed it! Where is Marianna?" I turn to Mateo with a flash of dark shadow, my hands on his shoulders, talons digging in but not piercing the skin.

"She lives, Adam. I brought her here this morning just to be safe. She's safely asleep in the guest room." I sigh and drop my head, leaning over Mateo as relief runs through me. Mateo is my rock, able to keep me calm in even the fiercest moments. He hands me another goblet. "Drink, my friend, you must."

Nodding, I take it this time, my talons shrinking back to normal as I take his newly activated phone from him. "Go pick up Kiera. Now, more than ever, we need to focus on the Forever Bound mates of my family. The Monroes would never act so blatantly if they did not see us as weak. They grow stronger by the day."

Mateo agrees silently, grabs another phone, and leaves me.

I walk over to the gothic floor to ceiling windows that overlook the dark drive to my mansion and watch Mateo leave in the limousine. I'm about to turn away when something in my soul stirs. There, in the shadows, walks Kiera. The lights of the limo light her up, revealing she's wearing nothing more than fitness leggings and a sports bra. She'd been running or jogging. In the dark, in this fog! The phone I took from Mateo shatters in my hand as fury overtakes me.

"She has no regard for her own safety!" I roar at the ceiling, but I have no time to scold her now. I grab another phone and quickly begin to call my brothers and warn them. Our city is under attack. Our rule of the city we raised from ashes and established ourselves may fall to the hands of the enemy if they do not find their women.

It's too late for me, but they still have a destiny to fulfill.

"Yes?" Brec answers his own phone, like he always does.

I go back to the window and speak as I watch Mateo usher

my vixen into the safety of my family home. "You've seen the news?" I ask, and my brother grunts.

"I've seen it, and I wish one day to burn their homes as they burn our city."

We growl at the thought, the predator in both of us reacting to each other.

"I know this is the last thing you want to talk about, Brec, but you must begin the search for your Forever bound."

I feel Brec sneer even if I cannot see him.

"My Forever Bound? I will never search for her. I will never kill as many women as Father did to find his Forever Bound, and all for nothing. I will not be enslaved to this madness, family and fortune be damned. We've led the vampire covens of this country for as long as vampires have been here. It will not change just because an upstart family thinks it should." My brother says every word with a snarl, and I know he wants to hang up, to finish the conversation there.

But I am the eldest and he respects me enough to wait until I declare we're finished.

"Without our women, we are weak, Brec," I say, my voice low. "Without the ability to continue the family line, more than just the Monroes will come for Sorin. We will soon be outnumbered by vampires who have successfully mated, and when they begin to produce offspring? We will lose. This is why they are bold enough to attack now." I clench my hand around the cell, telling myself I shouldn't break another one so soon. "You will set out to find her, Brec. More than fortune and power are at stake, our lives are on the line. Find her," I order, and hang up.

Without missing a beat, I dial Devion's number.

"Little busy right now, big brother," he answers, the moans of a woman in the background as Devion grunts. I hear a scream, and Devion drinking from the woman he's fucking. I growl with impatience and anger.

"Fuck!" Devion screams as he comes. "Well, wasn't her," he laughs.

"Is this a joke to you, brother?" I demand. "Women are not toys! You cannot just drain every woman you find attractive!" I'm fuming as Devion laughs and I hear a thud.

"Not everyone can hire a sexy little minx to do our work for us, Adam. My way is fun."

"And what if your way is killing the Forever Bound of your brothers? What if that woman you just tossed was *my* mate?"

I say the words through gritted teeth, knowing full well it wasn't my mate that just met her end.

"If she was your mate, you'd thank me. She was trash in bed. I'll find my Forever Bound, Adam, but I will do it my way."

Click. No respect from that brother. I worry about how rash he is, it's dangerous having a wild card like that in a powerful family.

My phone rings, and I answer in anger. "Devion if you ever hang up on me again I'll show you why you should fear your elders!"

"Woah woah, Adam it's me. Corbett." Fuck.

"I was just about to call you..." I say, apologetically.

"No worries. Devion can make the sanest man a monster in a matter of moments. I saw the news, and I've been looking for my girl. I'll never stop, I'll never let them win. Sorin City belongs to the Cadell family, and I pledge right here and now I'll die before I see them take the throne."

I grunt, glad to be hearing this. We are of a like mind, Corbett and I. Since the day he was born, I knew we were kindred spirits.

"I already tried calling Ever," Corbett continues. "But the phone just rings and rings. I imagine he's surfing the waves in the moonlight. I'll find him, my brother, don't you worry. I'll pull him back into the fold and get him to focus. One so young should not have this much pressure on his shoulders as we do."

I agree, and let him go as a soft knock at the door sounds through the room and Kiera walks in, sweaty and furious. She looks absolutely delicious in her maroon workout gear and I absentmindedly lick my lips, all thoughts of the pressure I'm putting on my brothers fading from my mind as she storms towards me.

"Who do you think you are? I went for a run! Just a run! Is fitness not something vampires do? I swear to god if you send Mateo to collect me like a belonging ever again, I'll scream!"

"You are absolutely beautiful when you're mad," I purr, and watch as her whole body blushes.

She looks away from me, frowning. "I haven't left the castle since the first day. I stay and I study and I sleep where I read and I continue when I wake up. I keep a bag in a spare room, but I don't use the room, I swear."

"Good," I smirk. "The only room I want you in is mine. The only bed you sleep in will be my own."

She raises an eyebrow at me, hand on her hip, and I'm reminded of that peasant woman long ago, who ripped her wrist to save her sister. The shock of the memory reminds me of what developing feelings for a woman can do, and I stroke the scar on my face pensively.

"Shall we get back to business, my Lord?" Kiera says saucily, walking over to a desk and completely ignoring my comment. "The seventeen hundreds, your second decade. Let's begin."

Something tugs in my chest. Something that's been buried for almost three centuries. The anguish and torment I went through, losing them... What I had to do to them and what they did to me...

I tamp down on the memories, knowing that if I don't,

they'll assault me of their own will. This is one story Kiera will never hear.

The scar on my face aches as it did the day I received it, as if the silver knife is slashing me all over again, and I grit my teeth.

It's time to continue this farce of finding my fated mate.

Not relive the fact I no longer have a Forever Bound.

CHAPTER 5
KIERA

Adam is pensive, looking away from me and touching the scar on his face. The jagged mark is an intrigue to me, and I hope we cover that story soon. I know the only thing that can hurt a vampire enough to leave a permanent scar is silver, but he doesn't linger on the scars from battles past. Only this one. And the way he looks at me as he touches it stirs something in my soul.

I walk away from him, leaving him to his thoughts and go over to the floor to ceiling windows where I saw him watching me only moments before. In the distance, the city lights illuminate the low-lying fog, giving the night a mysterious and ethereal glow. I place my hand on the cold glass, wishing there was seating here so I could look over the city while we speak.

As if he can read my mind, Adam drags a small red velvet love seat to the window and motions for me to sit. I smile at him and lay a hand on his arm in thanks. I wish I had time to change out of my leggings and sports bra, but I came in too much of a hurry to yell at Adam. I kick my running shoes off and curl up on the loveseat with my legs underneath me.

Adam is leaning on the window frame with his shoulder, his

legs crossed. The way the moonlight plays over his skin makes him look surreal. The shadows brighten and hide his curls in shadow, the light reflecting off his eyes and illuminating his irises, almost making the silver blue glow in the night. He squares his shoulders and turns to me, his shirt unbuttoned half-way and I can see the shine of his scars in the moonlight. He looks so severe, so dangerous, but for some reason, all I want to do is comfort him as if he's wounded.

Adam stares at me like I'm the most precious thing in the world, and I shift uncomfortably. Trying to remind myself of my true intentions here, trying to close my heart to him.

He walks to the door to the throne room and pulls a long golden rope and I hear a bell ring somewhere in the castle. Within moments, Mateo wheels in a cart laden with delicate hors d'oeuvres and sets a nearby table with them, pouring a glass of tea in the cutest blue lace teacup and saucer I've ever seen. Adam pours a crystal goblet of blood for himself, but when he approaches the table, he puts two sugar cubes in the tea and brings me the delicate cup and saucer.

"I don't know what you prefer to eat, so I ordered a bit of everything. Gourmet cheeses and meats, tarts and cakes, even escargot if that's what you like." I glanced at the table as Mateo leaves the room. There's even caviar with a special silver spoon lying next to it.

Adam hands it to me and I whisper thanks, trying not to blush. He retrieves his blood glass and lounges on the love seat next to me, his thigh touching mine, his arm on the back of the couch around my shoulders where he runs the tips of his fingers on the back of my neck in slow circles. I sip my tea, wishing my heart didn't stir every time he looks at me, wishing his thoughtfulness didn't affect me so deeply. I have to hurt this vampire, I have to doom him to a life alone. There's no room for affection.

I take my pen from behind my ear and set it to the paper,

beginning to write. "So, you change your life every hundred years. Don't humans notice that you never age? I could never forget your face if I tried."

"I do not deal with humans I don't employ. I like my privacy and being the ominous figure inside the castle." He taps the scar on his face. "As you said, I have a face easily recognizable so I stay pretty reclusive. When I do meet new humans, they look at me with fear in their eyes. As if my scar is some unspoken threat of violence towards them. So I employ the same families for generations. Mateo's ancestors gave birth in the castle even in the 1700s."

Adam cringes as he says this, as if he's revealed some bit of personal information he didn't mean to lead to. I tuck the information away and move on, noting to follow up on it later.

I can't help thinking to myself that it's a shame no humans were brave enough to know Adam, they missed out on something amazing. He's so brutally handsome, the scar on his face only emphasizes his beauty for me. It doesn't scare me, it intrigues me. I want to touch it, heal it, heal the pain that he carries with the jagged mark. Whatever caused that scar has scarred his heart as well as his face, and I want to know how it happened.

But I'm not here to ask those kinds of questions; I'm here to find his Forever Bound and kill her. Destroying his life and legacy. I bite my bottom lip and look away in shame.

"Every century has been about adapting to the times." Adam's eyes leave me and he looks out the window at the city, his gaze glossing over as I imagine he sees the city how it used to be. "It's important that we blend in, wear the proper clothes and act a certain way. Humans do not need to know we exist. I must appear rich in every lifetime, but not so much that the human leaders feel threatened by my presence."

"That all worked great until the Monroes appeared in your

territory, right?" I point out, and Adam's silver eyes flash and focus on me like hard steel cutting into my soul.

"With great power comes great competition. When you have such dominion over such wealth, there will always be someone trying to steal it from you. We were kings when the Monroes encroached on our land, but there cannot be an open vampiric battle in a town like there would have been in the dark ages, so we battle in the background. Secret assassinations, foiling of plans, destruction of property. Like they did with the club."

The hard and predatory way he moves as he speaks of battling them sends a shiver down my spine. Partly of fear, imagining the slaughter that humans aren't even aware of, but part of it is the heart stopping uncontrollable attraction I have to him. Power rolls off of him and I want to ride that power with him deep inside me.

I am what he speaks of, a secret assassin sent in this war of vampires. And as the power seems to swell inside him and he appears more and more imposing, I've never felt more vulnerable in my life. I stare at his hands, those gentle fingers that teased me last night would turn into sharp black talons if he knew my true intentions; he could rip me to shreds right here in this room and no one would know or care. I shift uncomfortably as his eyes devour me from my head to my toes and I clear my throat.

"So...uh...how do you prosper?" I say, trying to keep a tremble of fear out of my voice.

A flicker of amusement crosses his face and he smirks at me. "These days? Gas stations. In the past, stagecoach houses or brothels. The pony expresses even. When you're as old as I am and know as many humans as I have, they become very easy to predict. The addition of motorized vehicles only made it easier.

Every day humans flock to the place where they can make their transportation continue without a hitch.

"So I build them, my human employees run them. Mateo's grandfather currently runs my refineries and factories, keeping my businesses in business and running smoothly. Mateo's uncles and brother procure the blood I drink through donation centers that I also run. Advertisements for such centers are based in my clubs, gas stations, even the grocery stores I own. No other blood bank pays as richly as I do, and the humans come in droves.

"Does Mateo have any aunts? And females in his family besides Marianna?" I'm completely impressed by Adam's ingenuity, but it's women we need to discuss, not the countless men who work for him. I try to think about his servants, and it occurs to me I have never seen another woman in this castle besides Marianna who moved in yesterday, shyly giving me some scented oil she bought because it made her think of me.

"No, no women have been born to Mateo's familiar lineage since his original ancestors." Adam bites off his sentence, closing down that line of conversation like slamming a door. Mateo's original ancestors were women... That could be very important.

This means, however, that Adam's been surrounded only by men for centuries and centuries.

I huff in frustration. "If I didn't know from personal experience, I'd say you must be gay. Employing all these men for most of your long life."

His brow arches and the predatory threat from before takes a whole new air. His hand that had been making small circles on my shoulders suddenly wraps around the back of my neck and in a blur Adam is kneeling on the couch over me, pulling my head back to look him directly in his fierce and powerful face.

"Shall I remind you again how much I adore the female form? Gay..." He chuckles and undoes his pants with his other hand, the massive length of cock standing at attention already rock hard and dripping pre cum. "You think I could get this hard for a man?" He strokes himself slowly, and even though I fight it, I can feel myself instantly get wet and ready for him.

I breathe deeply, making my chest rise and fall seductively. I don't know what has come over me, but I have a savage need to fuck him. I set my notebook down and take the goblet from where he let it spill on the couch. It still has blood in it. He watches me, entranced, as I raise the cup to my lips. I grin at him as his cock twitches in anticipation of what's to come, and I spill the final drops of blood onto my chest.

Adam's nostrils flare and his eyes go wild. Too fast for my eyes to follow, he falls to his knees, ripping my legs from underneath me and throwing them wide open. He grabs my hips and pulls me to the edge of the loveseat. His fingers have turned to talons, his eyes reflecting the red of the blood on my chest as he crushes me against him. He buries his face in my cleavage, sucking and licking every drop of crimson off me.

His savage hunger makes me wild. The talons I feared so much are running down my exposed skin, impossibly gentle. I tangle my hands in his curls and he rips his shirt off, pulling me off the couch and setting me on the floor in front of the windows. He props my back against the window—he wants me to watch. The moonlight plays with the shadows and the muscles of his back as he lays between my legs like a panther going in for the feast.

Adam's talons hook under my sports bra and the fabric splits willingly beneath the sharp pressure. He shreds the clothes off me, running sharp lines down my legs and ripping the cloth as if it held enough resistance as warm butter. When I lie beneath him, completely nude, he rises to his knees, stroking his cock and watching me. I sit up, reaching for him; he's so beautiful in the moonlight, like an avenging battle worn soldier. I rake my hands over his chest, our eyes locked in the throes of passion that are soon to come.

Adam's taloned hands run through my hair, the sharp sensation causing full body shivers, and he takes fistfuls of my hair and draws my mouth close to his cock. "Taste how bad I want you, Kiera," he demands.

I'm completely entranced by the magic of this moment, no better than a sex crazed animal, and I slowly lick the very tip of his cock. I barely touch it, taking only the bead of pre-cum with the tip of my tongue.

I savor the sweet saltiness and relish in how his body shudders at the brief contact. I lick again, barely touching and teasing him as he teased me, and I sigh on his cock as I register he'll lose control very soon. I want him to, I want him to show me what I do to him, to take me right here and now, exactly as he desires. My eyes challenge him to do just that as I suck only the very tip of his head into my mouth.

With a gut-wrenching growl Adam lifts me, throwing me on the loveseat with my legs over the back of the couch and my head dangling down off the seat. I look at him, upside down, and his imposing, powerful body comes towards me. A claw rests on my mouth as he bids with growls of wild insistence that I open it. I've never been taken like this, and the wild nature of it has me begging for more. I open my mouth and he tilts my head down, pushing his cock slowly into my mouth, so deep I can feel him in my throat.

The position makes sense now. Me laying on my back has opened a straight channel into my throat, and I suck him like I've never sucked a man before. His hand, talons and all, trace lines on my body, hooking around my nipples as he presses deeper into my throat, the curls around his sex tickling my chin.

I reach around him, taking a hand full of his ass and pulling him deeper in my mouth.

I've always been worried that having someone so deep inside me would make me choke, but his pre-cum soothes my throat like a salve and I want every inch of him inside me. Adam sighs, gently pushing into my throat rhythmically. I hear him suck on his fingers and my hips arch in preparation as he sinks thick fingers deep inside me, hooking them and finding my g-spot without effort. I lose it, bucking against his hand and sucking him wildly, and he groans with pleasure as my moans vibrate my throat around him.

"Gods..." he chokes out. "You're so much better than I imagined. Your mouth is so hot...ugh... That's right, harder... good girl...suck my cock just like that." Adam leans over me, bracing himself on the back of the couch with one hand, and cupping my mound with his palm as his long finger stroke and probe, bringing me closer and closer to climax as I writhe in pleasure.

"Swallow every drop, vixen..." he groans, his thrust becoming insistent, his seed sets my throat on fire.

I swallow, my throat tightening around his cock and he roars at the ceiling, the pleasure too much for him to contain. Wave after wave come and I swallow, drinking him down, my body aflame with heat and need. I'm so close to my own climax, my whimpers around his dick telling him just how close, but he pulls his fingers out, pulls his cock out of my mouth, and pulls away from me.

I reach for him, shaming myself with a pitiful whine. "Adam, come to me... I'm so close. Adam?"

He walks away with an evil grin, then he sits on the marble staircase and strokes himself. Daring me with his eyes and his body to take what I want. I slide off the couch, getting on my hands and knees and prowling over to him. I'm angry that he would torture me like this, so I move slow, teasing him, licking his seed off my lips.

I stand on my knees in front of the dais at his feet and put my hands between my legs. I'll make myself come in front of him. I refuse to let him have it. He watches me rub my own clit, his cock twitching as I throw my head back and moan. I watch, entranced, as he sucks the taste of me off his fingers and watches me like a starving animal.

I'm so close, my moans wild as I buck against my own hand and as I feel my orgasm begin, he reaches out with preternatural speed, grabbing me before I can blink and pulling me up to sit on his face. I straddle him, knees on the top step of the dais, and ride his magnificent tongue. I'm coming, clenching and convulsing all over his face, screaming as he fucks me with his tongue. A normal human man would drown with all the juices coming out of me, but Adam? Adam doesn't need to breathe.

He buries his head between the folds of my sex as if his whole face could fuck me. He doesn't breathe, so he doesn't pull away. He's relentless and my body quakes as I come uncontrollably over and over. His hands, talons again, run down my back, scratching me. It doesn't even hurt. The pain adds to the pleasure, and I'm feral with need. I've never been fucked so thoroughly without a cock even being inside me. I've never felt such carnal wild pleasure. My heart is beating so fast I feel like I could die.

With strong, insistent hands, Adam grabs my hips and pulls me over his chest, sliding me down his body. His cock slides into my hot cunt like it was built to fit there, seating deeply inside me as if we're one piece. I gasp, face to face with him, his arms holding me tight as he grinds into me painfully slow and gentle. Our eyes lock, his hands tangle in my hair and mine on the cold marble floor as I take control and ride him.

Adam kisses me, his tongue dancing with mine as I being to

fuck him hard and wild. I wrap my hand around his throat and push him away, sitting up and riding him feral and fast, choking him, demanding he let me have what I want. His arms stretch out, gripping the marble stairs so hard they crack as he lifts his hips and fucks in time with my thrusts, harder and harder, until the most brutal cervical orgasm I've ever had rips through me.

I release his throat, riding him, screaming my pleasure so loud it echoes off the cathedral like ceiling.

My hands are in my hair, my curls cascading down my back, and Adam's eyes never leave mine. The stairs under his hands are crushing to dust, and I feel he's forcing himself not to touch me. There's worry in his eyes that he might crush me as the dais crushes beneath his power. As my orgasm wanes he relaxes, sitting up and pulling me close to him. I wrap my arms and legs around him as he stands, still fucking me deeply. He stands there, holding me up in the air, and his mouth goes to my jugular. His fangs scrape my sensitive skin, and I moan.

In sheer disbelief, I come hard and fast again. The idea of him completing the circle by drinking from me is so desperately intoxicating that I feel the words on my lips. 'Bite me' I want to demand, but his need to bite turns into a sucking kiss. He sucks my neck hard, his cock pounding into me even harder even though he's standing and the only thing supporting my weight are his strong hands.

I feel the bruise forming beneath his mouth, my blood gathering and begging to be released from my skin. With a roar, he comes again, his come exploding out of me, dripping on the floor as he pumps wildly, any semblance of control gone. I feel the sweet torture of our pleasure shudder through his body, enthralled and touched. This is just as powerful for him as it is for me.

He releases my neck and kisses my mouth tenderly. Gently,

he lowers me to the ground and his face hardens, a shadow replacing the haze of lust in his eyes.

Without a word, Adam leaves the throne room, leaving me naked and confused, dripping like a fountain. Through the craze and waves of pleasure, part of me feels disappointed and abandoned.

I sigh. I know I'll regret this, just like I did the first time. I know I should be angry at myself. I know Adam walking away was exactly what should have happened.

But my body still thrums with delicious tingles. My heart is purring like a satisfied feline. So I lay on the loveseat he moved for me, one arm behind my head and the other cupping my throbbing center, and fade off to sleep.

Regret will be waiting tomorrow.

CHAPTER 6
ADAM

"Why can't I control myself around that woman?" I say out loud as I lean against the door to the throne room.

"Dunno boss, but she surely makes you stand at attention!" I scowl at Mateo as he walks by with a stack of books, his gaze darting to my crotch. "I don't think I've ever seen you rise to the occasion like that." Mateo laughs as he walks away, completely unconcerned.

I watch my friend go without really seeing him. All I can think of is biting Kiera. I want to taste her blood on my lips so bad, it's physically painful. I clutch my throat, feeling so parched it's as if I haven't had blood for years. Like that time... after...

My fingers wrap around my neck, the nails digging in and I almost consider turning them into talons. I need the physical pain to chase away the hovering emotional pain.

I cannot let myself be vulnerable like that again.

I cannot let my guard down with Kiera.

I square my shoulders and steel my soul, channeling the heartless killer that I am. Kiera threatens to awaken my cold heart, and I must not let her. My fractured heart is too fragile, even after all these centuries of losing my Forever Bound.

I look off the way Mateo had left, the first time I met his ancestors rising unbidden in my mind. I try to fight it, try to suppress the agonizing moment where my destiny changed, but I find I can't fight it and my blood lust. My thirst for Kiera has made me weak.

And I have no choice but be thrust back into the past.

1732 BC

My country home is more of a country cottage than a castle. The house is a sprawling stone dwelling deep in a dark forest. Most would say it's creepy, haunted, but since the human women came here several months ago, they've brought life with them.

I stand at the gate to my home, taking in how beautiful it's become in the time I've been gone. The dead vines growing on my home are now rich with roses that climb the walls, the shingles on the roof have been mended, broken windows fixed, and a vegetable garden flourishes. Even the willow trees on the banks of the babbling brook seem to be filled with renewed life. The scents of rose, jasmine and gardenia mix to create a heady cocktail.

As I enter the gate, Carmen walks out the door. She's heavily pregnant, and with one look at me, she's terrified. She falls to her knees, dropping a basket full of wet laundry, and clutches her stomach. Anna hears the commotion and runs out. Fear crosses her eyes but she steps over her sister and holds a broom up to defend them.

"Stay away!" she yells at me, the fire in her eyes a reflection of her wild red hair.

I hadn't realized when I met them they both were ginger with startling green eyes. They were too filthy. The last time they saw me, I left them here with a trunk of gold and jewels and told them the home was theirs. My servants made them nervous, so I sent them back to the castle. They've been alone in the cottage for three months, undisturbed.

I hold my hands out to them, my palms open. "I am not here to harm you. I come to make sure you are prospering in your new home."

The broom falters in Anna's hands, but her eyes stay sharp.

Carmen, trying to regain her composure, reaches up and grabs her sister's skirts. "This is the one that spared us, I think..." she says in hushed tones.

Not for the first time, I'm reminded that the familiar traits of my father are strong in his sons. I step closer and they freeze when Anna raises the broom again. This time she smashes it against the stone wall, making the end a jagged stake.

"I will kill you, vampire!" she hisses between clenched teeth.

I step forward anyway, the stake pressing into my chest. She pushes as hard as she can and if I were human or the stake was silver, she may have penetrated my skin.

I grab Anna's face gently, forcing her to look into my eyes. A tingle runs through my fingers as I make contact, and I feel my heartbeat for the first time in my life. I'm startled, but I must focus. I look deep into her eyes, compelling her to obey.

"Anna," I whisper. "I am your friend. I am not here to harm you. I'm here to care for you and for your sister."

The air around us thickens, deepens, electricity popping as she fights the compulsion and I have to use more and more energy. Carmen stands, worry on her face as she begs me to release her sister, but we can't hear her.

Looking into Anna's eyes, I'm transfixed. Her face is framed by fiery red curls, her green eyes sharp and powerful. I brush my thumb over her trembling pink lips and her mouth parts. Her tongue darts out to lick my thumb.

I draw in a sharp breath as lust grips my loins. As emotion floods my empty heart. As destiny refuses to be denied.

It's over in that moment, and like a wildfire she's on me.

Anna's arms wrap around my neck and her lips press fearlessly to mine. I freeze as she seems to have lost all control. I look at Carmen through her sister's red hair and she's just as shocked as I am. The tense air evaporates, and against my own will, my arms close around Anna in a desperate embrace.

For the first time in my life, my cock rises. Anna is wild, moaning and ripping at my clothes, and I'm lost in the feel of her lips on mine. Her plump pink mouth tastes like warm sugar and honey, her tongue seeks mine and I fall to my knees. Electricity surges through my body at the brush of her tongue. She breaks the kiss, adjusting herself to straddle my lap as I sit on my knees.

I tangle my hands in her hair, our eyes locked, and she bites her bottom lip and moans, rocking against my hard cock.

"Can you feel it..." she says breathily. "Sweet heavens, it's beautiful. Amazing. And only growing stronger by the moment. I don't know you, but I need you. Take me. Here, now, at this moment." She unbuttons her blouse and her perfect pink tits spill out of her shirt and over her corset. She arches her back and my mouth closes over her nipple of its own volition.

I forget about Carmen. I don't know if she stays and watches as I shred every ounce of clothing from her sister and lay her in the dirt in front of the threshold of the home. Anna lies naked beneath me, her fire red curls between her legs dark with moisture. I shred my own clothes with just a flex of muscles and when Anna sees my cock, her eyes go wide and she raises her hips to reach mine. My body is like solid marble, unmarred by blemish or scar, and she looks upon me as if I'm a god in the flesh.

"Now!" she demands.

I do not disappoint her. I grab her hips, her head and shoulders still on the ground, and I sink into her roughly. She screams as blood covers my cock, and I freeze. Anna is the first woman I have ever been with, so I didn't know women bleed during sex. I watch tears stream down her face in her pain, but she grabs me and pulls herself up, wrapping her arms around my neck and her legs around my waist, pushing my throbbing length deeper, deeper.

Anna kisses me and her tears wet my face. I wrap my hands beneath her backside and push slowly in and out. Her tears of pain turn to moans of sheer delight. Soon, we're roughly grinding against each other, her blood stopping and clear white fluid replacing it. Every stroke inside her is like I'm home, every caress of her lips burns me like fire.

She bites me. *She* bites *me*. I roar, her ineffectual teeth don't break my skin but mine break hers. I can't help it. I bite her shoulder and she screams in delight. She tastes just like I hoped; floral, rich. She's hot as fire and sweet as honey. I've never had blood satiate me like this. Uncontrollably I spill my seed inside of her, shuddering in shock as I've never felt such pleasure as this before.

Anna moans and a flush of fluid mixes with my seed and I'm drunk on it. She leans back, hands in her hair, floating in the air as only my hands hold her above the ground. I watch her ride me, her juices soaking my own curls around my throbbing cock. I watch as my seed spills out of her, and I pull her close to lick the blood I spilled off her perfect breasts.

I know at this moment that she's mine and I am hers. I don't know why, or even how, but my soul connects with hers in a way I've only ever heard about. Does this mean...she's my Forever Bound? She kisses me, hungry but tired. I stand, her body still wrapped around mine and my cock still inside her.

I carry her into the home and she waves towards a bedroom without ever breaking our kiss. I lay her on a lavish four post bed and take her again and again until she fades to sleep, unable to stay awake a single moment longer.

I drink from Anna every day forward as we make love. Carmen doesn't understand it, but she doesn't come between us. I become more and more certain Anna is my Forever Bound, but I cannot bear to drain her and risk this pleasure for my greed.

Weeks pass and I become a constant in their home. Many nights I hunt for them and bring them fresh meat. We sit in front of the fireplace and I tell them stories of my past. Carmen becomes like a sister to me as she seems to understand the connection between Anna and I is inexplicable. As such, she accepts me as the head of household.

One night as they sleep, I tend the fire to keep them warm. Carmen has become more and more uncomfortable as her due date passes and she still remains with child. She has chosen to sleep in an armchair by the fire, her belly much too large for her to lie in comfort.

On this night she stirs awake, hands on her belly, and she smiles up at me. "Adam, come here," she says quietly.

I take a knee in front of her, reverent as I've never been so close to a life bringer. She takes my hand and sets it on her stomach and I feel the baby roll and kick beneath her skin.

I'm in awe. I press my face to her stomach and listen as the baby kicks inside her. Its tiny hand pushes my face away and I laugh. I truly laugh, a happiness and feeling of contentment I could never fathom fills my soul. This is my family.

"Adam... I need you to go... I need you to find a doctor. I

worry for my son; I worry that he does not come." I look up into her eyes as tears of sorrow and desperation flow down her face. "Please."

"I will go now. Let me wake Anna and say goodbye."

"No, you must not," she says urgently, her hands on my shoulders. "If you tell her, she will go with you. Adam, I do not want to face this alone."

I flee the house moments later, desperation in my heart. I will not let Carmen die. I will not lose the precious soul she carries.

How could I have known the danger I left them in? How could I have ever guessed what would unfold in the mere hours I was away?

I return the next morning in a horse drawn carriage with a doctor and a team of nurses, but there's not a single sound in the house. I burst through the doors, only to find the women I have grown so close to are gone. I try to focus, try to think, when a woman outside screams. I run towards the sound but I smell it before I see it, a trail of blood. I turn to shadow as I race away from the cottage, leaving the doctor and his menagerie behind. I can sense that the blood is Anna's, for it does not smell like Carmen's.

The trail ends at a shack in the middle of a field of wheat. I freeze, taking my normal form and crouching low to the ground. The wheat undulates like an ocean in the pale dawn. I hear a heartbeat coming from inside the shack, and I know it is Anna's. She's afraid, desperately afraid. I focus, trying to find any other small detail that will tell me if she's alone, but I hear and see nothing.

Racing towards the shack, sure that my love is alone, I burst through the door, splinters flying everywhere. Anna is chained to the wall, tears streaming down her face and her night clothes torn and bloody.

I rush to my love, registering the chains binding her are silver and I cannot break them. She throws her arms around my neck and sobs. "I'm so sorry, Adam, I couldn't protect her..."

I kiss her, holding her close. "Who has done this? Who dared to put a hand on my woman!"

The pale morning is rewound as dark shadows form around me, my rage boiling out of control. Whoever did this will pay, their descendants will pay.

Suddenly, there's a flash of silver and burning pain slices through my face. I stumble back, confused, raising my hand to my face and finding bright red blood. I can barely see out of my left eye, but I look up just in time to see Anna isn't chained to anything, she's only wearing a chain around her ankle.

And on the other end of the chain in her hand is a silver dagger as long as my forearm.

She looks at me in shock and fear, her hands trembling. But then her face tightens, hardens, and she lunges. The knife is aimed for my heart, but I catch her wrist.

"Let me kill you!" she sobs.

She's not nearly strong enough to overpower me, but my strength falters at the words and the knife pricks my chest. As the blood wells beneath the knife, Anna screams, her hand trembling as if I'm stopping her, not getting any further. I release her, take two steps back in utter shock, and she falls to her knees, wailing and keening for forgiveness. I didn't know humans could make a sound like that, a bone chilling loss, and my heart breaks for her. It doesn't matter that she just tried to take my life, I love her.

I fall to my knees in front of her, trying to gently lift her head up to look at me. "Anna, what's going on? Where did you get that knife?"

"They wore a red rose with silver thorns dripping blood... they took her. They said if I don't kill you, they will cut the baby from her belly as they cut her in front of me. I have to kill you! I have to save them! But...but I can't...I love you... Oh my god, Adam, I love you so much." Anna folds in on herself, huddled on the shack floor in the fetal position and crying. "I can't kill you, and I can't watch her die..."

I stand up, looking around, trying to scent anything; maybe even to hear a baby cry. I turn to ask Anna which way they went, to tell her I can save her sister, only to roar as I leap toward her.

But I'm too late.

Anna plunges the knife into her chest, burying it to the hilt.

Her scream will echo in my mind for as long as I live. I fall to my knees beside her, screaming for help myself, but there's no one to come.

Anna puts a bloody hand on my face, and I can hear her heart slow. I bite her wrist, and her face contorts in anguish. It's my last chance to save her. I know she's my Forever Bound, if I can just drain her, she will live. She has to live. I pull the knife out of her and suck viscously, trying to hurry before the rest of her blood is on the floor and not in me.

Anna is smiling at me now, a knowing look in her eyes that I will never unsee.

"They took her... to the... the town... Sorin town... save her for me? Save her baby?"

She coughs, and blood trickles down her cheek. I blink and try to wipe it away, but when I look again, her eyes are blank. Her heart has stopped.

I was too late. She didn't survive.

I roar at the ceiling, screaming for hours upon hours. The

pain is so great, I'm ready to die with her, but I remember her last words. I pick up her body, cradling her as we both turn to shadow, and I race for the Cadell Castle.

When I enter the throne room my family is there, each with a woman on their lap, feasting. I walk in, covered in blood and filth, the love of my life dead in my arms. I fall to the floor, crying over her body, telling them vengeance must be wrought.

In that moment, the war between the Cadells and the Monroes is born.

As a family of shadow we track down Carmen and her attackers, they had indeed cut the baby boy from her stomach and I found her dead on a butcher floor with a Monroe prince holding a knife to the baby boy as he held him by the leg. I remember nothing but shadow; the prince's body exploding in a spray of blood as my brothers rip him limb from limb, and the tiny face of the baby boy as I cradled him in my arms.

Around me, the bloodbath began.

That night, my family destroyed Sorin Town. I stayed by Carmen's side, holding her head in my lap while her son cried in my arms. Corbett came back just before daylight with a slave girl.

"This one is in milk, her spawn died to the Monroes," was all he said.

He sat in a dark corner, I could feel him mourn for me even though he said nothing. I lost who was meant to be my Forever Bound; my father told me that because her heart had been pierced by silver there was no way she would have survived.

Sobbing, I held the babe out to the young woman. She was scared to be alone with us, but as the baby screamed, her breast swelled and began to leak. She fell to her knees and took the infant from me, nursing him as she sobbed in fear and mourning for her own child. I moved behind her, cradling the slave girl against my body and wrapping her and the child in my arms.

"If you raise him, girl, you will live in the lap of luxury. Your family and his family for generations will be safe from vampires and protected as long as I live. You will want for nothing, ever, no sickness will touch you for I will burn it away. If you raise this child, this I promise you."

The young woman, who told me her name was Maria, agreed silently. She nursed the baby until they both fell asleep in my arms. I stayed awake all through the day, ready to rip anyone to shreds if someone dared harm my humans. I swore to myself to destroy the Monroe line, whether it takes days or centuries.

I snap out of my memory when my computer dings as an email arrives, the modern sound far too alien to be ignored. I frown when I see it's from an unknown address.

I scowl when I read the single line.

We will find her. And we will kill her. - M

My heart stutters again, wrenched by the same pain of centuries ago. The Monroes are wasting their time.

Kiera cannot be Anna.

I searched for her for centuries, in the same way my father searched for his Forever Bound once she was killed.

He may still be continuing the futile search, but I know the truth.

Once a Forever Bound is killed, then never reincarnate again.

CHAPTER 7
KIERA
EARLIER THAT DAY

Coming home to my grandmother's house is always a comforting experience, even with the Monroes watching our every move and keeping my family hostage. She has a quaint Victorian style apartment with loud red wallpaper covered in white roses, ancient Russian tapestries over the windows and in almost every corner you can see one of her collections of antique china sets. My Babushka is as old as Mother Russia itself. The deep lines of wrinkles on her face are like a map of the world, her lips no more than a crack that splits her face with a toothless grin every time she smiles. When she smiles? The whole world lights up. It's impossible to be sad around Babushka.

Which is exactly what I need right now.

When I arrive, my little sister and her daughter are already seated at the dining table and Babushka is serving them borscht with a side of pirozhki, the steam still rising. Babushka throws her hands up into the air and cheers in Russian when she sees me, and my sister Emma gives me a big hug. Sweet Jenny is too focused on her cheesy pirozhki to notice me.

"Privet sestra!" my sister says as she pulls back from the hug and we share a meaningful glance. "Are you well, Keira?"

My younger sister stares at me intently, conscious that the burden of protecting the family has continuously landed on my shoulders. Unlike myself with my dark hair and green eyes, Emma and Jenny have blonde hair and blue eyes. Jenny looks like a clone of our late mother, but Emma and I have different fathers and she gets her delicate soft features from him.

"Everything's fine," I assure her, but Emma simply raises a brow. I sigh. "We'll talk later. I'm starving! Babushka, is there enough for one more?"

Babushka rolls her eyes at me, waving me away as if I've insulted her. She was already setting me a place. We sit at the table and begin to eat, the familiar rhythm of family around me. Emma tells us that Jenny's now ready full novels, pride glistening in her eyes. Jenny nods enthusiastically, her mouth too full of good Russian food to add much. Babushka nods at all of it, her wizened face scrunched in thought.

"Nichto v zhizni ne sluchayno..." she begins.

My mind silently translates the Russian she speaks in, 'Nothing in life is a coincidence,' even as I know this is probably another one of her musings that don't always make sense.

She nods to me, and nods to the food. "I knew you would come, for you must come, at this time," she continues. "Last night I dreamed of a home, a blood drenched town, horrible shadows fought in the streets."

Emma and I glance at each other, knowing this may take some time. Babushka has always had an impressive imagination. Jenny continues to slurp her borscht, not even paying attention.

"People die, but the shadows who hurt them? They die in other shadows. I hear a man wailing, I hear a baby crying. I see a bleeding man hand me a child, and I know I must love him as my own."

She pauses, gumming a bite of borscht as she is deep in thought.

"I see you Kiera, I see you in danger and I see you in love. I'm confused, it makes no sense. Nichto v zhizni ne sluchayno..." Babushka drifts off then, into her own world.

I find I've been holding my breath. She knows nothing about our situation with the Monroes, we've kept her out of it so she wouldn't worry. But she knows about the shadows...

Emma reaches across the table and takes my hand, mouthing 'nothing is a coincidence.' Even though Babushka doesn't know, she knows. She worries.

My family is why I must do this, why I must find and kill Adam's Forever Bound. If I don't, the Monroes have made it clear what they will do to us. I look at little Jenny as she talks with Babushka in Russian. She's only seven, but Babushka's been speaking to her in her mother tongue since she was a baby. They smile at each other, red borscht dripping down their chins as they eat messily on purpose.

My stomach heaves. In my mind it's not the soup dripping, but their blood, as they're beaten and killed when I fail.

Emma sees the look on my face and she nods to the kitchen and I follow quietly; I can't bear to see them right now.

"Kiera, you look like a ghost. Is everything really alright? Have you found her yet? I can't imagine having to kill someone ever, but having to work with the vampire and get to know him first?" She puts her hand on my shoulder. "I know this isn't easy for you. Your heart is huge and you wouldn't hurt a fly unless you had to. I'm so sorry this has fallen on you."

I wipe away the tears that prick my eyes and I hug my sister tight. "Everything is not okay, everything is going sideways." I heave in a shuddering breath, the truth refusing to be denied.

"Emma...I think I have feelings for him. Every time I'm near him it's like I can't breathe, my chest hurts, my heart hurts. I have no idea how I'm supposed to betray him! He's the most kind and caring man I've ever met, and he's a vampire! He's nothing like the Monroes, not even a little bit."

Emma shushes me as I begin to cry in earnest. I lean against her, resting my face on her shoulder and just cry.

"Come with me..." she says after a few moments. "I drew Jenny a bath for bed, but I think you need it more than her tonight. Let the warm water soothe you, just relax. I lay out some of my pajamas for you and you can sleep here tonight, okay? He won't miss you for one night, will he?"

I think about last night, about our rough and passionate sex in his throne room. I think about how I want him to bite me, but mostly I think about how he left me alone as if I was nothing but a whore.

As my sister leaves me in the bathroom, I stare at the steaming bubble bath in the stand alone clawfoot tub. The room is cloudy with steam and the mirror is completely fogged over. I undress, wiping the mirror with a hand towel to look at myself. I have bruises everywhere from where he gripped me just a little too hard. But my neck? My neck has a bruise in the shape of his teeth. I thank god I wore my hair down today as I step into the too-hot bath and let the sting of the water take my mind off of that man.

If I'm nothing but a whore to him, then it will never happen again. I'll find his Forever Bound and kill her and be done with it. I refuse to be used. I sigh as my body submerges in the water, leaning my head back on the cast iron tub and closing my eyes. Outside the bathroom, I hear Babushka and Jenny playing backgammon loudly with many whoops of joy when one of them wins.

Unwillingly, I begin to fall asleep. As my consciousness

relaxes, I see Adam's face in my mind, his harsh lines, his possessive gaze. Images of when he tied me down and tasted me until I couldn't come any more quickly follow, heating my blood. My hand slips between my legs of its own accord and I rub gentle circles around my clit like he did with his tongue. I remember his hungry eyes as he looked up at me with relish and squeezed my breasts. My eyes flutter closed as I squeeze the same breast, just like he did. I'm quietly moaning, rocking against my own hand as I fantasize about Adam and all the things we've done together.

I realize with a thrill of pleasure that he's never bent me over and taken me from behind. He's never pulled my hair, making me arch my back so he can kiss me while he fucks me so hard I can't walk when we're done. I orgasm powerfully as I imagine it, as I imagine him biting me and drinking from me as he spills his seed into my pussy, into my mouth, I want it everywhere. I moan loudly into my towel, trying to muffle the sound when there's a knock at the door.

"Kiera? You left your phone on the table. Someone named Marianna says she needs you? She's texting her address... She says it's important."

I race down the stairs of Babushka's apartment building in my sister's bunny pajamas and matching slippers and call Marianna. When she answers, I know something more than normal is wrong. Her voice trembles, her words are sharp and quick. She sounds terrified.

"Kiki, I don't know what to do... The sadness is drowning me and I can't call my brother... I don't want to admit it... I left the castle, being there was making it worse. Something about Adam sparked it! I don't know why, he's so gentle and kind.

Kiki... I don't wanna live like this... I need to cut. I want to end it. Kiera, I want to die. Please, I need help!"

I'm in tears myself as I reach my blue Prius and climb in. I'm racing down the road with her address in GPS before I know it, running red lights and nearly causing accidents at every turn.

"I'm on my way, Mari, please don't hurt yourself, okay? I don't want to lose you. I'll be there soon, we'll work this out. Promise me you won't hurt yourself, okay? Promise?"

The line goes dead, and my panic rises. As I pull up to Marianna's building, I see a crowd. People are pointing, screaming. Six floors above ground, she sits on the edge of the roof. I can hear her anguish from here as she cries. She's cutting herself, screaming, "I can't do it, I can't do it anymore!"

"Mari! Mari stop! I'm here! You have to stop!"

She sees me and reaches out, almost like she'll jump to get to me faster. I race in the building, taking the stairs two at a time. I don't feel the stitch in my side, I don't feel my lungs burning. Marianna is going to jump. I have to get up there first!

I burst through the roof door and see her standing on the edge, blood flowing freely down her arms and wetting the ledge and her shoes. She turns to look at me and the anguish in her eyes nearly stops my heart.

"I'm sorry, Kiki. I can't live like this anymore..."

She goes to step off the building, but I launch myself forward, gripping her blouse. With strength I didn't know I had, I yank her back and we tumble to the ground. We struggle as she pushes against me, screaming for me to let her go, screaming for help, anyone to help. Although I wear a few strikes to my torso, I manage to move us away from the ledge. Toward safety. Throughout it all. Marianna is thrashing, shielding herself from blows that weren't coming.

"Mari!" I crouch over her, trying to protect her head as she thrashes, almost as if she's having a seizure.

Suddenly she stills, looking at a spot over my head. "Let me die..." she begs, tears streaming down her face. "I can't live like this. Don't save me, let me die..."

Her eyes flutter closed as she loses consciousness, and I sag, relieved. She's alive. I frown as I take in the wounds on her arms. I still need to get her downstairs and bandaged up before she bleeds out.

Before I can try to drag her, a man with red hair and pale skin bursts through the door to the roof. Tears fall from light green eyes.

"I only left for an hour... Mateo made me promise to watch her. I went to get tequila!" The man's pudgy, with a beer belly and beard, and his Scottish accent is so thick I can barely understand him. "You must be Kiera, I'm Roger. Her neighbor." He gently picks Marianna up, the love in his eyes obvious. Just as clear as the fact that the love is unrequited. "Follow me, I've got a first aid kit ready in her apartment."

Roger is so gentle with Marianna, the tenderness he shows makes my heart clench. She lays limp in his arms, her head lolling and her blood dripping, although it's slowed. When we get to her apartment, I'm surprised by the color and glow of everything. It looks like a Latin paradise; everything has an air of the exotic and there are tiny fairy lights strung up on the roof. I feel as if I've walked into a Cantina, there's even fresh tortillas and carne asada set up for a feast.

I sit on a red couch with a crocheted blanket over the back and reach for Marianna. Roger lays her next to me, her head in my lap, and proceeds to care for her injuries.

"She has these terrors," he tells me quietly. "She says she feels like she's in another time. Says she's in a stagecoach stopped at a railroad station when someone rips her out. She doesn't know what's happening, but she hears laughter and feels searing pain. It's dark, but she can feel people biting her."

Roger pauses, holding her now bandaged arms in his hands. His eyes are wet with tears and he trembles. "You saw her calm? I've seen that so many times... Someone saves her, heals her. She never sees his face..."

"He has dark hair, pale scarred hands..." Marianna mumbles, cuddling closer to my stomach and grabbing a handful of my white camisole for security. "He smells like blood and hatred, fury and passion. He puts me on a black stallion and slaps the beast away so it runs and runs. I look over my shoulder and watch him rip those men limb from limb, and I see he has fangs and dark claws. His eyes seem to glow red as he watches me leave..." Mari's eyes fly open and she looks at me. "Kiera I don't know what scares me more, the attack or the creature that rescued me." She cuddles close, pulling her legs up into the fetal position as she falls asleep again.

I run my hands through her hair and Roger strokes her back. Outside, the sun is going down, and something in my soul stirs. I know a man like she describes, Adam. My mind drifts back to Babushka, 'nothing in life is coincidence'. Just like her, Marianna has memories she can't make sense of. Trauma from a past life...trauma where Adam saved her.

My hands freeze in Mari's hair. Their paths have crossed more than once. I'm holding Adam's Forever Bound in my arms, I'm sure of it.

A wave of unbearable sadness overwhelms me, and tears fall even though I bid them not to. I'm mourning Adam, I'm mourning what I will have to do to Marianna, and suddenly touching her becomes too much to handle.

"Roger, why don't you take Mari to her bed?"

Roger nods silently, lifting Marianna from my lap. She's asleep again, but as he picks her up she wraps her arms around his neck and nuzzles close. There's a moment where I can see Roger's heart stop as he squeezes her tightly, fighting the urge to kiss her. I follow them to the bedroom and pull back an Aztec patterned blanket for him to lay her down. He sets her down on the far side of the bed and crawls in after her. He curls his body around hers, spooning her and stroking her arm gently. I pull the blankets over them, sitting on the edge of the bed.

"Marianna has my number, call me if you need me..." I say quietly.

Roger only nods, taking a deep breath through his nose and smelling her hair. Before I leave I put their food away, growing more and more angry with Adam. He must have known this whole time it was her.

Marianna is his Forever Bound.

The bastard's been toying with me.

CHAPTER 8
ADAM

We will find her. And we will kill her.

Although the email shouldn't matter, it's on a loop in my head. Maybe it was because I was just thinking of Anna, but it births a fierce protectiveness. A raging drive to protect what's mine.

Even though I no longer have a Forever Bound.

The door to the throne room flies open and Kiera storms in, fury flushing her face. She's wearing pajamas, by the looks of it. Soft bunny print pants and a white camisole without a bra, bunny slippers, and a look on her face like she could murder me where I stand.

She storms towards me, her glorious breasts bouncing as she walks and yells something about Marianna, but all I can think of is bending her over my desk and pulling those bunny pajamas down...

We will find her. And we will kill her.

Rage fills my soul and shadows form around me as my fingers lengthen to talons. I rise from my desk and she cowers, actually cowers away from me. She apologizes, terror filling her eyes, but in a flash of shadow she's in my arms and we're dashing through the castle faster than she can see. She screams and clings to me and I can feel her tremble. Yet I can't stop the overwhelming drive surging through me. It's primal. Almost animalistic.

I have to protect her. I won't let them hurt her!

Desperation clouds my mind as we descend deeper and deeper into the castle, until finally we arrive at a twenty-foot door embedded in the stone beneath the castle. I rip it open and slam it closed behind us. Sealing us in complete darkness. I press Keira against the door, smelling her, taking in every ounce of her. She cannot see me but I can see her, I can see the terror, the confusion.

I can smell Marianna's blood on her and I have an idea what had her so furious. But I don't want to talk about my non-existent Forever Bound. I want Kiera. And if my being associated with me puts her in danger, then I will stop at nothing to protect her. Right now, she's all I can think about. I fall to my knees, pulling her pants down slowly. She tries to protest, but once my mouth closes around her curls all she can do is moan.

In the pitch dark, Kiera's skin glows like the moon. She cannot see me, but to me, she's glowing like a goddess. I lick her clit hard and slow, tasting every inch. Tasting lingering soap and a smell of lavender that doesn't smell like her soap at all. Her skin tastes of incense and Russian food, my mind briefly flashes back to handing Mateo's ancestor to the Russian woman all those years ago. She tastes like I remember that woman smells.

All thoughts leave my mind as Kiera's fingers wind in my hair, and she begs me to penetrate her. I'm not done tasting her, so I let her pull feebly as I sink two fingers deep inside her center and curl them, finding her g-spot as if it had a magnetic pull. She moans, grinding her hips against my hand and my face. I let her rub her clit up and down my nose before I clamp onto the sensitive nub with my mouth and suck, flicking her clit with my tongue simultaneously. She's coming already, fast and wet, and without realizing what I'm doing, I bite down.

Kiera screams, in pain and in pleasure, and the taste of her blood mixes with the taste of her sex. I feel drunk and my head spins at the heady cocktail. I didn't mean to pierce her skin but the taste of her on my mouth is intoxicating. I suck once, twice, savoring the taste of hot coppery blood with her signature honey sweetness. I know I must stop, even as I feel I've never tasted blood before she was on my lips. I lick the wounds, sealing them.

I lost control. She's not my Forever Bound but I drank from her body anyway. I stand slowly, shame filling me at the same time as her blood lights me on fire from the inside out.

"Adam…" she breathes. She reaches for me but I step back and her hands flail in the darkness. "Adam…"

She's begging now. I watch her in the darkness as she takes the rest of her clothes off, standing there naked, she shines. She turns, braces her hands on the door, and backs up. Sticking her bare ass out to me.

"I know you can see me, Adam…" she teases, gasping as she reaches between her legs and rubs her own clit. "Can you really stand there and deny you want this?" She dips her fingers inside her sweet cunt and moans so seductively I nearly come in my pants.

I watch her fuck herself, listening to her moan. She's already close to orgasming again. She's so close, knowing I'm watching. She's moaning wildly, pleading with nothing but the sounds of her desperate need.

I unbutton my pants slowly, stroking my rock-hard dick as it throbs. My cock fights my will and shame, pulling me unwillingly forward, unable to resist her magnetism. Kiera starts to come and I push myself hard and fast inside her, gripping her hair in a fist savagely and fucking her hard and rough like I know she wants. Her cunt tightness and spasms around my length, her moans now shrieks of pleasure. I pull her head back and kiss her shoulder, her neck. I bite her again.

"Yes! Adam, yes, let me feed you..." she moans, and I drink freely. Feeling my body come alive with every swallow.

I come fast and hard inside her, her cries making me lose my mind, and I reach around and grab her vulva. She will come on me again, and she will come on me now. I release the bite and bite the other side of her neck, rubbing circles around her clit as I fill her with wave after wave of my seed. I feel her tighten, her body stiffen, her screams rise, and we come together.

Kiera's cunt is so tight I can't thrust anymore, she's trapped me inside her. I feel like I belong there. I lick the bites on her neck, healing them without any scars, and as she releases her hold on my throbbing cock, I pull out of her. I pick her up and walk through the pitch-black room, laying her down on a magnificent sleigh bed covered in animal furs. We sink into the cloud of furs and I push myself back inside her from behind, filling her completely to the base of my shaft, holding still. I want only to be inside her, to be one with her.

Forever Bound be damned. Kiera is my only priority.

"Mine..." I say out loud, gently biting her earlobe, and Kiera goes completely stiff. As if she remembers why she came here, no doubt to do with Marianna. It doesn't matter. I scratch her neck with my teeth. "You're mine..." I growl, pulling her tighter to my chest, thrusting inside her once for emphasis.

"But I'm not..." she whispers, her voice small and trembling. I can smell the salt of her tears as she starts to cry, her shoulder shaking.

"You're mine if I say you are mine. My Forever Bound doesn't matter now. I choose you!" I declare, but she pulls away from me forcefully.

I let her go and stand, lighting candles around the room and revealing mountains of gold and jewels, rubies and emeralds, diamonds and gilded swords, all in heaps of piles surrounding the black oak sleigh bed. Even the bed is gilded with gold and diamonds.

Kiera gasps as she sits up and looks around. She pulls a lush wolf fur to her chest, covering the body I've claimed as mine. I step forward angrily and rip it off of her, pushing her down on the bed and crawling over her. "Mine!" I roar in her face, pinning her arms above her head and licking and kissing her from her neck down, insisting that she's mine with every touch of my lips.

"I can't be yours..." she sobs, and I bite her inner thigh and make it hurt. She shrieks and fights me, but my grip on her leg can't be broken. "I can't be yours because Marianna is yours!" she chokes on a sob as I lick the bite.

Kiera cries into her hands, sobbing for Marianna, for some guy named Roger. Even her blood tastes like sorrow. I lick my lips and grab her hips, pulling her back to my cock and rubbing the length of myself against her clit. I take her hands from her face, pinning her to the bed.

"I already told you, Kiera," I growl, my words dripping with venom and anger. "Marianna is not mine. I know this without a shadow of a doubt." I plunge into her again, watching her face go from sorrow to sublime pleasure.

"You saved her..." she gasps between moans as I fuck her. Every time she speaks, I fuck her harder. If only I could fuck her into obedience. "Stagecoach...past life...she was attacked... Monroes..." Her words fade to unintelligible moans as she comes violently.

"Impossible. Mateo has no female ancestors, besides the original woman." I do not release her, I do not stop plunging in and out of her. This isn't the real reason I know Marianna isn't my Forever Bound, but I can't tell Kiera the truth. She's here to find my fated mate. I can't risk losing her.

First, she has to understand that none of that matters anymore. Only she does.

"Mateo's male family members had to have wives, mothers, or their line would have dropped out of existence... Uhhg-gnnnn..." She comes again, and I grin from ear to ear, enjoying the way her body reacts to mine. "The Monroes, they were draining her...you killed them all...you sent her off on your stallion."

I freeze, my cock going instantly soft inside her. "How do you know this?" I demand, pulling out of her and pacing the treasure room. I remember that night, they were trying to kill her, drain her. I ended them all and never saw the woman again.

"Marianna and Roger told me." Kiera sits slowly, gingerly. I can see that I hurt her with my love making. "Those flashbacks she has, the ones that drive her to hurt herself? They're memories of her past life. She remembers you, being afraid of you, even though you were her savior. That is how I know." Kiera slides off the bed, and my nostrils flare as my seed drips down her thighs.

Gently she puts her small hands on my face "It was a brief moment in time, during the first millennia of war with the Monroes."

I put my hands over hers. "There are many memories of that time I would rather forget." I pull away from her, walking over to a throne and sitting on it, head in my hands.

"Just like the story of Mateo's original ancestors? The story you refuse to tell me?" She walks over and sits on my lap. She kisses my neck, snuggling close to me. "The journal for that year...all the pages are ripped out." She looks up at me and traces her finger down the long scar on my face. "That's how you got this? Mateo's original ancestors."

I tremble, I can't help it. No one has touched that scar but me since the day Anna sliced my face. Not since the day my Forever Bound died in my arms.

Just like Kiera touched the heart I thought was long dead.

But if she learns I have no Forever Bound, she could run. She would have no reason to be by my side.

I need more time.

"How I got this scar is inconsequential." I stand and reach for her, but she pulls her hand away from me and starts collecting her clothes. "I do not want Marianna or whoever else you think is my Forever Bound, I want you!" I bare my teeth at her and roar, grabbing her forcefully and holding her.

"That's just too bad, isn't it? Vampire!" She hisses back at me, baring her human teeth as I bared my fangs at her. "I am not *yours* and I never will be. You just use me! All you care about is my cunt!" She thrashes against me, pummeling me with her fists. "Let me out of this crypt, I have to go get Marianna. You'll taste her and you'll know." She turns a fiery gaze at me, her eyes shooting daggers into my soul.

"You will never taste me again, Adam. I've found your Forever Bound. It's Marianna. There's nothing you can do about it. I forbid you to touch me. You have a woman waiting. Now open this door!" She pushes on the door and it swings open. I forgot to lock it. I was too absorbed in her, needing to taste her.

My heart shatters as she runs away from me, off into the darkness of the castle alone.

She makes me feel more alive than I have in centuries, and I only have her lifetime to convince her to be mine.

CHAPTER 9
KIERA

I make my way blindly through the bowels of the castle, using nothing but the scent of fresh air to guide me. I can't stop crying and my eyes hurt from it. I sob as I stumble in the dark, pausing often to slide down a wall and cry in earnest. Why can't it be me? Why can't I be his Forever Bound? Killing myself would be easier than killing Marianna.

When I finally stumble out of the castle hours later, the sun is rising. Shaking, I make my way to my Prius, and once I'm inside my car I pull the visor down to look at myself in the mirror. Bruises formed where Adam bit me, where he tasted my blood at last. A shiver of pleasure climbs my spine at the memory. There are no wounds, no way to remember his bite. There will be no scars, and I find that sad.

My phone rings where it's sitting on the passenger seat and I jump. I must have forgotten it here. I clear my throat and wipe my face. I don't know the number, but it's a video call. When I answer, there's a man sitting in the shadows. I can only see his hands.

"Have you found her, slave?" an evil voice asks and my blood freezes in my veins.

I recognize the coat of arms on his cufflinks, the Monroe leader has called me himself. His fangs flash as he leans forward into the light, and my terror reflects back at me from the shine on my phone.

"I'm close!" I almost shout, fear roaring to life.

Thaddeus Monroe is the opposite of Adam. He's blonde with short hair, his dark eyes look almost black, and he radiates evil and murderous intent.

"Close isn't good enough, slave," he sneers, and I begin to tremble. I can't tell him about Marianna, I have to save her somehow.

"My other human slaves tell me that Jenny's school lacks security... It would be so simple to go in and eliminate her. It would look like a school shooting, slave. I have children who would do it, even without compulsion."

Hyperventilating, I lean out my door and vomit violently.

"That's right, slave... She will be the first. Every day you fail me after I have her killed, I will deliver you pieces of your family that I will rip off them with my own teeth. Or maybe, maybe your sister is the Forever Bound to one of my sons... Shall I have them drain her, drain her while you watch?" Thaddeus licks his lips, but his gaze freezes on my bruises. His voice goes from evil to downright menacing.

"Never let him drink from you again, slave!" he shouts, and my tears renew again.

"How... How can you tell?" I stutter, and he rolls his eyes.

"I am older than that fledgling, I know a vampire's kiss when I see it. When a vampire feeds on a human it creates an unbreakable bond, he will be able to sense you. The more often he feeds, the easier it will be for him to compel you. He could compel you to reveal your true intentions."

I grab my neck, terror shaking me to the bone.

"If it's just the vampiric kiss you desire, slave..." Thaddeus adjusts his phone to his trousers and he strokes his hard cock through the fabric. "I could have kissed you long ago... I could kiss you tonight, drain you dry, and set your sister on your path after I fuck you to death."

His evil laugh fills my car, and the last thing I see before he hangs up is his dick as he pulls it free and strokes it, coming on command on the phone.

I scream and throw my phone to the back seat of the car. I grip the steering wheel with a death grip and scream, shaking the car violently with my fit of terror. They're watching my niece, they'll rape and drain me and my sister. I know Marianna is Adam's Forever Bound. I have to do this, I have to kill her. I have to protect my family. Screaming again, desperation and longing cracking my soul in two, I peel out of the castle grounds, driving without any idea of where I'm going.

I'll kill myself, I'll drive into the ocean. No, I can't! If I die, they'll use my sister! I slam the steering wheel, driving recklessly. The twists and turns of the country roads blur, nothing matters anymore.

I have to kill my friend to protect my family, there's no other choice.

With a numb sense of clarity, I realize what I have to do. There's an apothecary not far away, I'll go there for poison. It'll be painless, her suffering will be over. That's what I have to focus on. Her suffering will be over.

I call Marianna from the beach, telling her I have a surprise. I'll be over tonight. I tell her to dress beautifully, we'll be going somewhere special. As the phone clicks off, I fall to my knees in the ocean and sob openly. Babushka believes in ghosts and reincarnation, if I kill Mari and she ends up a spirit I want her to be dressed with dignity and pose. Not fighting for her life and covered in blood.

The apothecary asked me no questions; he passed me a vial

of extract of yellow oleander. "Drink this, and you will die. It is final, and I do not condone suicide, so you must know there will be no coming back from this." I let him believe it's for me, and with tears streaming down my face, I leave. I'll mix it with champagne... Maybe I will drink it with her. End our suffering together.

Hours later, in my own sparsely furnished apartment, I mix the poison with the champagne. I know what I'll do, I'll tell her how Roger feels about her. We'll get drunk on the first bottle of champagne, she'll be happy. She'll be in love, there will be no fear. She'll get so drunk that when I change the bottle, she won't know the difference. She'll drink it and I'll leave, leaving Roger to find her in the morning.

As the sun rises I lay down in my bed, sobbing. I haven't known Marianne long, but her soul touches mine in ways I haven't expected. She reminds me of Babushka, and I know that if given time Babushka could help her. Her age-old wisdom is a balm to any soul.

In a perfect world, I wouldn't have to kill Mari to protect my family; my family could protect her. In a perfect world, I would be Adam's Forever Bound and he could save my family from the Monroes... In a perfect world? I could have his children...

I fade to sleep, dreaming of children with his strength and dark hair. Hating myself the entire time for dreaming of beautiful things when tomorrow I'll take everything he stands for away and destroy his family's legacy.

I sleep through the entire day, there's no point in going back to Adam. I know his Forever Bound, there's no need to research more. As the sun sets behind the skyscrapers of Sorin City I rise, watching the sunset from my apartment windows. I know what I have to do tonight, and I know what will happen if I don't. I need to harden my heart. An image of Adam holding me close and kissing me slips into my mind and I force it away.

I don't get to love him; I get to ruin his life.

I find my skimpiest sequin red dress, six-inch red stiletto high heels, and do my hair up in curls. My makeup is dark, alluring, and sultry. I grab the bottles of champagne and leave my apartment, barely registering my surroundings, none of it matters. Men gawk at me, women stare in awe and some in jealousy. As I slip into my Prius a man catcalls, and I pause and stare him down.

He's a good-looking guy with only one thing on his mind. He's coming home from the gym it looks l like, and as we make eye contact, he tries to approach. I envy him, his simple life. He probably isn't capable of what I have to do tonight, he probably couldn't even fathom it. I shake my head at him, but wink. No need to destroy his confidence.

As I take my seat and start the car, I call Marianna on my car's bluetooth. It rings four times and goes to voicemail. With a frown, I leave a message. "Girl! You gotta get ready. I'm taking you out! Girl's night! Just you and me! We'll drink until sunrise and forget all our troubles. Dress in your best gettin' laid attire, I'll be there in thirty minutes."

As I hang up, I almost vomit. I'm too good at lying. She'll be waiting for me excitedly. We'll have a wonderful night, and just before daylight, she'll die.

The drive to Marianna's takes longer than planned. It's a Friday night and the streets are packed. People are celebrating, it must be a holiday I've forgotten about. They roam the streets hooting and hollering, everyone drunk out of their minds. I realize with a pang of guilt that this has my motive making even more sense.

Marianna's apartment has a pop-up bar on the sidewalk, drunk people laughing and shoving each other. The roads are packed with people just having a good time. I smile and wave, dancing with people as I pass. Men grab me and spin me around. I laugh and try my hardest not to hit anyone with the champagne bottles in my hands. The joy in everyone is overwhelming me, and it only deepens my sorrow, feeding it just because I know that right now, I'm the antithesis of everything they're feeling.

Soon, I'm at the steps to Marianna's apartment building, the revelry behind me. At least we won't have to go too far to party. The elevator to Marianna's floor seems to not even move as time holds still, my heart seems to stop beating. The dread sinks in and my stomach drops out. I vomit in the corner of the elevator.

As the door opens, I wipe my mouth and plaster a smile on my face. Stepping out of the elevator like nothing's happened, I walk directly to her apartment. Except the door's open. Roger's door is open, too. A new dread sets in as I see the door to the roof is waving in the wind. I feel like puking again, all that partying and I didn't think to look up. To see if Marianna was having another spell. I drop the champagne bottles and they shatter, but I don't care anymore.

I race to the door, kicking off my heels just in case I have to catch her off the edge again. In the back of my mind a little voice asks why I would try to save her, why not just let her end it the way she wants. It solves both problems. Tears stream from my eyes when I realize that I could never have killed her. I love her. I love Adam, I can't do this to either of them!

I burst through the door to the roof and freeze, ducking back behind as fast as I can. There, on a picnic blanket lined with candles, are Roger and Mari. Naked in the moonlight. Making love. Roger's on his back and Mari's riding him slowly, lovingly as their hands trace lines on each other's skin with a tenderness that makes my heart ache.

I watch longer than I should. I watch them kiss. I watch Mari orgasm. I watch as Roger sits up and wraps her in his arms like she's made of glass. On Mari's hand, I see a delicate diamond ring. My heart stops.

I was coming here to kill her and now she's engaged to a man who loves her more than anyone in the world ever could.

I back away from the door slowly, tears streaming down my face and ruining my makeup. I can't kill her. Which means I can't protect my family.

Clutching my chest as I walk back to the elevator, I can hardly breathe through the sobbing. I fall on the floor of the elevator, kneeling in my own vomit, and keen uncontrollably. I've failed them all... Babushka... Emma... Little Jenny...

They'll all die because I couldn't follow through.

CHAPTER 10
ADAM

The day passes without a single word from Kiera. I can find her if I choose to. I will trace her scent and track her down. My soul yearns for her, there's no way I can ever not have her in my life, Forever Bound or not. I pace the throne room, becoming more and more irritated as the hours pass and she doesn't come home to me.

The scent of a woman fills my nostrils and I rush to the door, ripping it open and looking eye to eye with Marianna. She's startled, and she takes a few steps back, recognition flashing in her eyes as she remembers me as the shadow that saved her in her last life.

"Oh... It *is* you..." she whispers, her hand rising to touch my scar. I recoil from her touch. I don't want it.

"Can I help you, girl?" I ask, my voice harsh.

"I... I just wanted to see for myself..." she stutters. "To thank you for saving me before...even if it wasn't me... Ever since Kiera saved me from the rooftop, it's all been coming back to me." She pauses and swallows hard. "She's saved me before."

Before I can ask her what that means, she lifts her chin and continues.

"I slept with Roger," she announces, as if I care. "It felt like our souls clicked... Even as I realized why Kiera's been so interested in me. It only makes sense...that it would be me...so just do it! Just find out!"

Marianna raises her wrist and slashes it one final time.

"I'm not suicidal anymore," she says, a strange mix of relief and sorrow flashing across her face. "Kiera helped me see my memories for what they are. If I'm your Forever Bound, then let's do this, right now, right here. I'll bear your children but I won't give up Roger, we're engaged... I imagine you won't give up Kiera."

I push her hand away roughly. "I've tasted your blood, woman. Don't you remember? I've saved your life many times in this life alone."

"You've never swallowed," she counters, and forces her wrist against my mouth. "Drink. Prove it now," she demands.

There is a fire in her eyes, just like Carmen's all those years ago. Flashing my fangs, I latch onto her wrist, wanting to prove to her, to Kiera, that they're both wrong.

I drink, and her blood tastes absolutely foul. Just like all blood since I tasted Kiera. It's a cruel joke. I swallow and wipe the taste of her off my lips.

"There. See? Just like I told her, you're not mine."

Marianna's eyes widen. "How...how do you know?"

My shoulders sag, the truth now too heavy to bear. I should've told Kiera and I resolve to do exactly that. "My Forever Bound died when I found your family all those years ago," I say, licking the wounds on Marianna's wrist, healing them for the final time. "It seems we only get one chance to find them."

Relief washes over her face, quickly followed by a frown. "Have you seen Kiera? She was supposed to come by last night and never did. Her phone goes straight to voicemail—" She lets her voice trail off as I fade to dark mist. I shove past Marianna, nothing but shadow now. Did she ever leave the castle? Is she lost here?

As a shadow, I search every nook and cranny of my home, scaring the humans in my employ. I search the entire estate, but there's no sign of her. Just the tire tracks and burned rubber she left on the driveway as she left me the night I bit her.

"Did I kill her?" I demand out loud, everyone looking at me like I've lost my mind. I drank from her too greedily. She could have fainted from blood loss, driven off the road.

I couldn't live with myself if that were the case...

Mateo rushes to me, putting a calming hand through my shadows and I take solid form. I look at him, desperation and fear contorting my face.

"You didn't kill her, I watched her leave. She was fine."

I grab him, my talons sinking into the flesh of his arms. "If you saw her, why didn't you stop her!" I scream in his face, and Mateo winces.

I drop him. I swore to never hurt anyone in his family. I fall into a crouch, head in my hands, and I cry for Kiera. The first time I've cried for a woman since...

"I have her address, Adam." Mateo says calmly, straightening his suit. "I can take you there."

As he speaks Marianna brings one of my cars around, a Cadillac Escalade; pure white. She hops out of the driver's seat with a grin on her face. "The prince always shows up on a white stallion. Go get your princess!" She tosses Mateo the keys. "Sorry for stealing the keys, but I figured once Mateo calmed you down, you'd want to get going as fast as you could."

I barely register a word she said as I snatch the keys from Mateo and jump in the driver's seat. Mateo hardly makes it in the car before I peel out, leaving Marianna coughing in a cloud of dust.

"You should know," I say as I speed around corners, Mateo gripping the dash of the car with white knuckles. As long as he's been alive, he's never seen me drive myself anywhere, much less at these speeds. "Mari's pregnant. It's very new, she'd have no way to know, but I could smell it. Taste it in her blood."

Mateo is shocked for barely a second before his face lights up with glee. He grabs his phone to call her, but my hand grabs his arm and stops him.

"Let them discover it themselves, a child—especially a first child—is a momentous moment for every couple. Don't take the surprise from them. I only tell you so you can watch her. Make sure she's safe. I can taste hormones, Mateo. I can say for almost certainty that she will have the first girl born to your family in many, many years."

Mateo laughs, his eyes glazing with tears of happiness. "Leave it to my sister to break years of tradition! A girl? Who would have thought!"

CHAPTER 11
KIERA

I cry uncontrollably as I walk like a ghost through my apartment. My mind is on a permanent loop of hopelessness. There's nothing I can do. I thought once that maybe if I take my own life they would leave them alone, but I can never be sure.

If I take my life, I can't protect them at all.

I stop when I see the essential oil blend Mari gave me a few days ago, the one I left here because it made me feel too guilty. I read the ingredients, my hands trembling so hard I have to grip it with the other. Rose, jasmine and gardenia. I suppose it sounds nice, although it's not a mix I've ever tried. The gift itself is more symbolic than anything. The friend who bought me something because she thought of me, the one who just found love, is the person I have to kill.

Still clutching the small bottle, I keep moving, hot tears scalding my cold cheeks. Reaching the bathroom, I decide to have a shower. Maybe it can wash away some of this listlessness. I need to act. Not feel sorry for myself.

I turn the water on as hot as I can, walking into the scalding stream as if I'm punishing myself. The spray of droplets is all that's needed to bring me to my knees. I collapse, a wail climbing up my throat then echoing around the glass walls, wrapping me in sorrow. The small bottle slips from my numb fingers and smashes on the tiles, the overwhelming scent of rose, jasmine and gardenia filling the small space along with the steam.

I sob, grief erupting from me and I shudder as I inhale, drawing a lungful of the scent.

Instantly, the world around me fades. Replaced by a movie that's impossibly real.

Because it's a life I've lived before.

I'm in a small hut, earthen floor beneath my bare feet, mudbrick walls around me. A hearth is to my left, a cast iron pot hanging above the glowing coals. My sister is leaning over the pot, her wild red hair tucked up in a bun, one hand on the soft swell of her stomach as she hums quietly. The sweet scent of berries fills the hut.

Despite the rough surroundings, contentment and peace are all I feel.

Until our father storms in, eyes so wide the white seems to swallow his face. "I'm sorry," he gasps. "I did the only thing I could think of to save you..."

Roman soldiers march in behind him, smashing a chair and kicking over the table.

All my father does is cower against the wall. "I sold you to the Cadell empire. If I didn't, the Monroes would've killed you along with me. Go with them, go!"

The soldiers seize us, throwing us over their shoulders and running out into the night. From beneath my own riot of red curls, I watch my father run after us, only to be stopped by a blonde man who steps out of the shadows. A grin flashes briefly, revealing sharpened canines, right before he rips my father's throat out with his teeth.

I scream, and the soldier throws me over the back of a horse and gags me. I cling to the saddle as we ride into the darkness, exchanging a terrified glance with my sister as she's taken away in a different direction.

Carmen, my heart screams. *How has this become our life? Our end...*

I ride with my silent savior for a full night and day. He never speaks. We never stop. The horse never falters and neither does the soldier. When we arrive at the castle, he heaves me off like a sack of salt. My whimper is cut off when I see my sister being dragged by the hair up the steps and into a monstrous castle.

Fueled by a fresh wave of terror, I thrash and fight. I will not be a vampire's meal! Never!

We fight the soldiers all the way to a throne room, where the dim sound of arguing is pounding into my sore skull. I'm tired, filthy, my sister is sobbing and begging. We're dumped onto the ground and I look up to see we're surrounded by three men, vampires, all with pitch black hair and royal garb. An older one, graying at the temples, sits on a throne.

One of the vampires approaches us. His gaze falls on Carmen and he smiles, exposing fangs as his movements become predatory.

He's going to drain her in front of me! I try to lunge at him, but his own brother knocks him away.

I freeze, terrified as brother battles brother. I crawl to my sister, shielding her head and her stomach with my body. I won't let them hurt Carmen. I refuse to let her die. My mind scrambles; so much has happened in just a few days. It wasn't long ago we were picking berries in preparation of making jam. My fingers are still stained red with the juices. Red... blood... I look at Carmen, desperate to defend her baby, and I rip my own wrist open with my teeth.

I stand up, raising my bloody wrist above my head. "If

you're going to kill me, my Lords, just get it over with. Spare my sister, she is with child. Do not end two lives this day. I sacrifice myself to your thirst!"

The fighting intensifies, no doubt fueled by the scent of blood. One of them splits away, becoming little more than shadows as he streaks toward me. I brace myself, ready to die for this, only hoping that it will save Carmen and her baby.

Except the vampire grabs my sister and I scream, flinging myself on him. He shoves me away as if I'm an insect. Then I'm flying, exploding with pain as I hit something, then there's nothing but blackness.

When I wake we're in a stone cabin, just my sister and me. She tells me the good brother saved us, that we get to live here now unbothered. The following months are beyond peaceful. I watch my sister swell with child and I adore every minute. We've never been happier, never felt safer.

That is, until he comes back.

I walk out the door and see him there, in all his glory. My heart skips a beat. In the moonlight he looks ethereal, like an angel descended upon us. The same protective fury I felt in the castle engulfs me as I tell him I'll kill him. I even break my broom to stake him to death.

But my body tells a different story, my body screams for him.

He comes closer, and I wonder if he can hear my heart beating out of my chest. His scent overwhelms me and something in my heart clicks into place. Destiny takes over.

Fate smiles with satisfaction as souls find their mate.

I let him take my virginity there in the dirt. The moonlight washes our skin as fireflies buzz around. It's the most magical moment I've ever experienced... When he bites me, my heart screams for joy. I love him instantly, at that moment. I know he's my future. My everything.

My sister doesn't understand, but she doesn't interfere. Adam and I make love insatiably. A family and lifetime with this vampire are all I want. It's all he wants.

Until one night, when everything changes.

I hear my sister scream. I think her labor has started so I rush out of my room realizing too late that Adam isn't with me. In the doorway are five blonde men, blonde like the man who killed my father. They grab my sister, bite her, drinking from her as they pull her out of our home and away.

One man walks towards me, an evil grin on his face as he strikes me. I fall in a heap on the ground, pain exploding through my skull, blood rushing from my brow.

Another man picks me up and licks the blood off my face. "I can see what he likes about her!" he laughs, and throws me to the third man.

They push me around, slapping me, kicking me, until I scream and beg them to stop. I beg them for my sister. I plead that they don't harm her. The leader kneels in front of me, grabbing me by my hair and pulling me up to my knees.

"You love your sister, slave?" he coos. I nod feebly. "That's so sweet, so very sweet." He looks back and laughs with the other men.

"My name is Thaddeus Monroe and I killed your father. If you ever want to see your sister alive you have to do something for me, slave. You have to kill Adam Cadell."

I gasp in horror, but it only makes him grin harder. He holds a silver knife out, a silver chain dangles to the ground with a shackle. With quick movement, Thaddeus shackles me, then uses the knife to slice my chest open. Blood flows freely as he stands, grabs the chain, and drags me out.

They drag me to a shack, chain me up, and remind me what I have to do. They made sure I left a trail of blood for Adam to follow.

I steel myself, alone in that cabin, waiting for him to find me. I know what I have to do, so when he comes and he kisses me, I strike, slicing his face. His beautiful, unmarred face. Hatred fills me, hatred for myself, for the Monroes, for everything I have done.

Yet despite everything I do, Adam doesn't care that I hurt him, he loves me. He refuses to turn his back on me.

He's my soulmate...and I have to kill him.

Without thinking, I plunge the knife into my heart. I can't do it. I can't take his life.

He's the only one who can make this right. "They took her... to the... the town..." I whisper, coldness spreading through my limbs. "Sorin town... save her for me? Save her baby?"

And please, Adam, forgive me...

I jerk awake in the cold shower. I can feel hot blood pouring down my chest but I'm not bleeding. It's then that everything makes sense, why I'm so drawn to Adam, why I can't help but love him.

I am Adam's Forever Bound.

And I have been for millennia.

CHAPTER 12
ADAM

We weave through traffic, through pedestrians, the streetlights flashing and blurring. Centuries ago I would have plowed them down, not even caring who I killed to get to her. I'm tempted to do so now as they cross the road illegally. The steering wheel cracks under my hands. I can't waste this time! Something could be wrong, something could be keeping her from me! Rage fills me and I fill the Cadillac with black smoke as the idea hits me that maybe when she left me she was taken by my enemy...

"It's there, fifth floor, apartment 505."

I see where Mateo points, and before he can blink I'm out of the car and gone. As a shadow the humans do not see me, the night does not illuminate me. I scale the outside of the wall like a wild animal, feral with the need to find my woman and protect her. I reach her window and look in. There's sparse furniture, take out littered on tables and benches, dark everywhere as if no one's been there for days. I almost howl with frustration when I see a crack of light through a doorway. White tiles are visible, telling me it's the bathroom. And a pale hand is stretched out on the floor. She's laying on her bathroom floor, she might be dead!

I shatter the window with barely an effort, flooding her apartment with my shadow. The faint scent of rose, jasmine and gardenia fill my nostrils, bringing back memories of the day I returned to the cottage, the day I discovered Anna was my Forever Bound, but I shove them away.

Kiera is my world now. I don't need a Forever Bound.

I step through the bathroom and see her asleep on the floor, completely naked. Her eyes are swollen, her body curled into the fetal position. I crouch down beside her, gently stroking the hair out of her face, and when her green eyes open and meet mine, my soul seems to shiver.

Tears like diamonds start rolling down her face and she reaches for me wordlessly and I take her into my arms. I sit on the tiled floor, her naked body trembling in my arms as she sobs. She clings to me desperately, as if I might fade away, as if I'm not even really there.

"Kiera, my love, what happened? What's wrong? Where have you been? Why didn't you come back to me?"

She freezes and sucks in a shaky breath, she turns her eyes up to me and the look on her face breaks my heart. "Do you love me?" Her voice is barely a whisper, doubt clouding her eyes, uncertainty making her whole body tremble.

"I love you, Keira. I love you more than my life. I love her more than my family. I love you more than I ever thought possible. Forever Bound be damned, I want *you*," I say fiercely, knowing it's the truth. I'm leaving the Cadell empire vulnerable by not having a Forever Bound, but I don't care. Kiera is all that matters.

I hold her close, kissing her lips tenderly as a new wave of tears overtakes her.

"If you love me, take us away. Let's go get my family, let's go somewhere, anywhere! I want you to meet them. I want you to love them as much as I love you. Please...please... Adam, please..." Her fingernails dig into my collar, her desperation palpable.

I place both my hands on her face and kiss her. "I'll take you anywhere you want. I'd go to hell and back if you asked me to."

She smiles, but new tears form in her eyes. She pulls away from me, standing up and running to the living room to snatch her phone off the table.

"Emma, you, Jenny and Babushka need to come to my place. Don't pack anything, just come. As fast as you can! If anyone asks, tell them we're having dinner at my place. Tell them I did it, we're celebrating." She turns back to me as she hangs up. "You have a helicopter, right? Of course you do. There is a landing pad on the roof. Can we go today? Can we go now?"

I watch her, standing there naked with nothing but the moonlight to light the room. She's running from something, she's absolutely terrified. I pull myself up off the floor and shoot a text to Mateo, and throw my phone out the window I broke. I take her phone and I throw it out the window, too.

"I don't know what you're running from, but no one is going to hurt you. Ever again. Your family is my family. You. Are. Safe." I say each of the last words separately, enunciating every word for emphasis. "Tell me what you're afraid of. I'll destroy them. I'll call my brothers and we will make them extinct. Tell me, Kiera."

She's trembling, biting her lips in fear, and she walks away from me, into the kitchen, and hops on the counter. "I'll tell you, but right now? Right now, I need you inside me. We have an hour before they can get here, and I want to spend every minute making love to you, Adam."

What she doesn't know is my text to Mateo was to find her

family, get them to my house and on the helicopter. When the helicopter arrives, they will be here and ready.

I unbutton my pants faster than I ever have, shedding my clothes and walking over to her like a lion on the prowl. There's no time for foreplay, no time to mess around. I grab her hips and plunge into her body hard and fast. She screams, moaning wildly already. We fuck hard and fast on the counter. She bites me and my hands crush the cabinets behind her. I bite her back and feel like her blood is the only sustenance I'll ever be able to stomach again.

Even as the passion pounds through me, I only sip. I will not risk her life. She means more to me than any Forever Bound ever could, and no one else in the world matters but her and what makes her happy.

All it takes is a handful of wild strokes. We come too fast, too hard, clinging to each other desperately. Growling, knowing I'll never get enough of this woman, I sink to my knees. I pull her hips to my mouth and eat her out until she's screaming for mercy. She can't have my seed spilling down her legs in front of Babushka, that would never do. I clean her greedily, hungrily, and every time she orgasms, I suck the fluid from her before it can even drip as the whoop whoop of the helicopter gets closer and closer.

I know Mateo will be knocking soon, so I stand and kiss Kiera more gently than I ever knew I could. She's limp and breathless and gorgeous. And she's finally accepted we can't be apart. I walk away from her, going to her closet and grabbing the first dress I see, a long black Maxi dress, and help her put it on. We look at each other, words not necessary as we prepare to leave this life behind.

And build a new one, together.

When the knock comes at the door I rise, wash my face and cock off with water from the sink, and wash her mound with ice cold water too, watching with a primal thrill as she shrinks back from the cold. She's mine. Mine. As I dress, Mateo opens the door and I lose control of myself. I hiss at him and raise my claws to attack, grabbing Keira and putting her behind me all in one swift moment.

Mateo doesn't even flinch, he just smiles at us. He can smell sex just as easily as any human can. "The heli is ready. I took the liberty of ordering clothes for them to be delivered to the house already. I hope you don't mind, but the chateau in the Alps seemed the most fitting. It's being prepared for our arrival."

Kiera looks at me shocked, "They're not here yet, Adam! We can't go without them!"

"They're here, milady," Mateo answers. "I had the police intercept their bus on the freeway and they escorted them to the castle. They're waiting in the helicopter above. Are you ready to go?"

I watch Kiera as her face goes from fear to sheer delight. She smiles up at me and I swear my heart beats in response.

I scoop her up into my arms and carry her out of her apartment for the last time. She doesn't know it yet, but she's never coming back here. I'll make her my wife in the Swiss Alps, and no one will separate us again.

The way Kiera's sweet family light up when they first see the mountains rising in the distance is enough to make any man happy. I can provide for her family, my family now. Whatever they fear will turn to dust in my path. Any opposition will be a red mist of blood as I pass. This is my family, forever. God help the person who threatens them from this moment on.

As we fly over my villa, I relish as they all suck in a sharp breath. The four-story wooden home is enough to take anyone's breath away. Almost every exterior wall has floor to ceiling windows, the house itself nestled against a sheer rock wall on the side of the mountain. A welcoming glow radiates from the golden light of the massive fireplace in the main room.

I cringe inwardly as I realize none of us are dressed for the snow. Those things don't matter to a vampire who doesn't mind any temperature. I look at Mateo and he only nods, showing me his phone. They all have appropriate clothes being loaded in their personal closets. He swipes and I see my master suite covered in furs, fancy floor length jackets for both me and my love laying on the bed in preparation for us as my maids scramble about to prepare.

Satisfied, I put my arm around Kiera's shoulders as she cranes her neck to see everything at once. She and little Jenny are like mirror images of each other, hands on the glass staring out in awe. Emma and Babushka do not take in the scenery, they hold hands and watch me.

Babushka's eyes take me in knowingly. "Tvoye serdtse znayet yeye."

"She says, 'Your heart knows hers,'" Jenny translates, and I nod.

"I know, sestra."

I smile at her, I speak nearly every language. I've had lifetimes to learn them all. Emma is startled, but she smiles. It's like they know, like they understand this is their life now. They seem to be delighted. Emma watches her sister in my arms, and I can feel the happiness and love she feels for Kiera. Kiera turns to me and smiles. There's only a hint of darkness lingering in her eyes as she throws her arms around my shoulders and thanks me.

That night, after dinner, I retire to the master suite to find Kiera naked on the deck outside the room. In the moonlight she looks like an angel, her curly brown hair spiraling free down her back and blowing in the frigid wind. She turns to me, pale nipples hard as rocks, and smiles, even though her eyes are haunted.

"What are you doing out here in the cold?" I laugh and throw my arms around her.

"I've only been out here a minute. I saw the hot tub and I thought..." She reaches down and strokes me through my pants.

I'm instantly hard, as if the mere suggestion is the most erotic thing in the world. I pick her up and take her to the bubbling hot tub, setting her delicately in the warm water. Kiera shrieks in delight and sinks her body into the water and watches me like a siren in the ocean while I strip and lower myself in the water next to her.

She doesn't waste a moment. As soon as I'm seated, she's on top of me and I'm inside her. She feels like heaven as her hot cunt tightens around me and welcomes me home. I kiss her mouth, her neck, I lick and bite her nipples. I don't want anyone else, legacy be damned. My Forever Bound died all those years ago, and nothing could be better than this.

I lean back, arms on the sides of the hot tub as she rides me. Her head back, her body undulating. Her nipples are so hard I know they could break glass. I watch her, enraptured, as she takes her pleasure from my body. I reach up and trail a finger from her lips all the way down her body, marking the very center of her.

When I reach her hips, I grab them with both hands and pound into her in motion with her body. She screams and laughs, her arms around my neck as she pulls me close. I bite her breast, drinking from her ravenously, drinking too much... I stop myself.

"You can do it... There's nothing I want more." She looks into my eyes and pulls me closer, begging me to bite her again.

I refuse, I will never risk her. Even if it means she will never bear my children, even if it damns my legacy and I watch her wither and age. One lifetime will be enough, rather than this being our last night together. I shake my head and grab her, flipping her over on her knees and taking her from behind.

The shock of the quick movement completely derails her train of thought. I reach around her hips and cup her mound, my middle finger sinking between her lips and rubbing her clit as I pound into her savagely. We fuck and orgasm so many times that by the time Kiera's done, she's too weak to walk. I carry her gently into our rooms, towel her off, and lay her naked on the fur-covered bed. I sink down behind her, pushing my still hard cock back inside her. She moans in protest, but I shush her.

"I just want to be inside you as you sleep. I won't move."

She sighs and settles in against me, evilly clenching and unclenching her vagina as I finish talking, but before I can scold her for being a tease I hear a delicate snore slip out of her perfect mouth.

I bury my face in her damp hair, absorbing everything about her; from the way she smells to the texture of her hair. Without realizing it, for the first time in centuries, I fall asleep with a woman in my arms.

The shutters begin to close themselves as the sun rises, and I see a hint of red on the horizon. Red, like blood, as the sun rises.

It matters not, I have everything I will ever want.

CHAPTER 13
KIERA

I wake with a start as the shutters open on their own over a beautiful red sunset. Adam feels me wake and his hands instantly cup me between the legs. I am so blissfully happy, so utterly content. His fingers find my clit, sink inside me, and hook around to play with my g-spot. I turn my head to him, raising my arm up and around his head to kiss him, but it's not Adam.

It's Thaddeus Monroe.

I scream and scream and scream. Thaddeus's hands are on me, shaking me, calling my name. I blink and sit bolt upright in bed…it's a nightmare.

Adam is there, holding me, calming me, kissing my shoulder. I melt into him and sob. "Shh, my love, it was just a dream… Just a bad dream…" He tilts my head up and brushes my lips with his. I have to tell him. He has to know what I've done… what I was sent to do.

Who I really am, that I'm his Forever Bound.

Then he can bite me, make me strong. I can make sure I don't repeat the mistakes of my former life. We can protect my family.

"Adam," I say, holding his face so I can gaze into his eyes. "I need to tell you something. "I'm—"

Mateo bursts through the door, blood dripping from his brow, and falls on the floor. "Monroes!" he gasps. He's carrying Babushka and she's deathly pale. "They killed all the servants, they have Emma... And Jenny..."

I fly out of the bed, running to Babushka as he sets her on the ground. She's still alive, but barely, her body covered in bite marks. She looks at me, but she reaches for Adam.

"I save da baby...lifetimes ago save da baby for ya...save my babies now..." A ghost of a smile plays on her lips. ""Priyatno videt' tebya, moy drug."

Her hand drops, and her eyes glaze over. She's gone, dead.

"No!" I scream, throwing my body over her and sobbing uncontrollably. I was supposed to stop the killing. I wanted to save them.

Adam is roaring, but it feels like background noise as he speaks to Mateo. "Why would they target her family? How does that accomplish anything? They're just humans! They couldn't possibly think that harming them would get them anything!"

I look up from where I'm curled around my grandmother, his words starting to sink in.

"They said it's because they ran, that Kiera broke her word," Mateo says, wiping the blood from his confused brow.

"Adam!" I gasp, knowing I've left this too late.

The window behind us shatters, and in the light of a red moon we watch as Thaddeus Monroe himself walks through the shattered panes. He's flanked by a dozen men, black bat wings flapping behind each and every one of them.

"Kiera..." Thaddeus practically sings my name. "We had a deal, my dear. You were supposed to find his Forever Bound, not fuck him. I told you if you wanted to fuck a vampire, I was available! Then you take my prisoners and run? I'm disappointed."

Adam turns to shadow and lunges, except two black winged men stop him. He fights them wildly, but they pin him against a wall with silver daggers poised at his ribs. Another grabs Mateo, and all I can do is sit there dumbly on the floor.

I look at Adam and cry as the realization dawns on him and the love in his eyes turns to hatred. "This is what you were running from? Or did you bring me here so I would be alone, away from my family and defenses so they could kill me?" he snaps, and I flinch back, unable to form words.

Thaddeus steps up behind me, grabs me by my hair and hauls me to my feet. He wraps his arms around me and I freeze with terror. I'm not scared of what's going to happen next. I'm scared that Adam will never know the truth.

"Adam—"

Thaddeus bites my neck savagely, ripping the skin and making me scream in agony.

Adam thrashes against the vampires holding him, his eyes torn between betrayal and murderous intent, and another vampire joins his two captors, holding a knife to his throat.

Thaddeus inhales deeply, his nose running over my tattered skin. "She came out here hoping you could save her and her family. The silly thing. See, I hired her to find your Forever Bound and kill her, but she failed." He laughs, licking a drop of blood off my neck but not healing the gaping wounds.

Adam roars in fury, thrashing against the men holding him and glaring at me like he'll tear me limb from limb.

I shake my head. I can't have betrayed him. Not again.

"I found her..." I whisper, and everything in the room goes instantly quiet. I look at Adam, my vision blurring. "I was going to tell you everything, but I had to be sure we were safe. I had to be sure you really loved me, I—"

"What do you mean, you found her?" Thaddeus roars, his

hand closing around my throat. "You bitch! Where is she? I'll kill her myself!"

I reach for Adam, desperate, unable to speak as Thaddeus crushes me. A fresh wave of agony has tears spilling from my eyes. My heart is shredding with far more violence than my body.

Adam freezes, his eyes going wide with shock as realization hits him. He looks down at Babushka, back at me. He's crossed paths with my ancestors alright...

"I was... Anna..." I choke out.

Adam sags as his knees go weak. "Anna," he whispers.

Thaddeus begins to laugh. At first it's just a quiet chuckle, but it rises to a booming roar. "You? You're his Forever Bound? I've had you all this time?" He cackles uncontrollably, fondling me in front of Adam.

Adam slowly rises again, his chest inflating. I can see everything adding up for him. Our connection, our desperation to be together. The sheer magnetic pull that we could never deny.

"Kill him, I want her to watch him die!" Thaddeus screams and his men move to impale him to the wall.

"No!" I shriek, pushing away from Thaddeus and snatching a silver knife from one of the men holding Adam before they can react. "It's me you wanted dead, remember?"

I put the knife to my throat and Adam thrashes.

All the Monroe men freeze.

"Well, if this isn't poetic!" Thaddeus sneers, "Isn't this how Anna died, Adam? She took her own life rather than watch you die?" He laughs and reaches for me but I back away, skirting around the room, around his men, trying to draw the attention away from Adam. "But I have Adam now, I can kill him and keep you for myself. You do taste quite amazing. I could make it last weeks before you die. Come, doesn't that sound better than dying right now? We all know how much you like your vampires."

As he cackles and Adam thrashes, I've worked my way around his men and out to the balcony. They all watch me, knowing for certain I'm no threat and they can stop me before I ever cut my throat. With my back to the porch railing and a sheer cliff drop behind me I look to Adam one last time.

"I'm so sorry, my love. Had I known sooner, maybe it could have been different. I wish you drained me last night like I asked and you would have seen. I love you..."

Without another word, I throw myself off the railing backwards, plummeting down the sheer cliff. Hopefully he can escape while they're shocked. Maybe he can kill them all...maybe...

Shadows explode out of the room as furious fighting breaks out. I close my eyes, accepting death, wishing it was different even as I wonder if I'm fated to live life after life, sacrificing myself so Adam can live.

A small part of my shattered heart is okay with that. Giving my life for his is enough reason to exist.

But I stop suddenly. My eyes fly open as I register I haven't hit the ground, I've hit someone's chest. I scream as I realize I'm being flown away by one of Thaddeus's sons. All around me are bat winged men, even Thaddeus, blood smeared across his cheek.

Behind me, I can hear Adam screaming, but it grows more and more distant. The cold air chills me to the bone and I pass out from sheer terror.

CHAPTER 14
ADAM

I only have time to heal Mateo's wounds before I call my family. I'm frantic. I'm overflowing with rage. I'm terrified.

Kiera was my Forever Bound all along, but my guarded heart refused to consider it. The possibility of being hurt as deeply and endlessly as I was when I lost Anna meant I refused to make myself vulnerable like that again.

And now, I might lose Kiera anyway. The scar running down the side of my face flares white hot. Her betrayal doesn't matter. It never did. Just like the first time, she was the Monroes pawn.

As the dial tone rings in my ear, Babushka's final words float through my mind.

Priyatno videt' tebya, moy drug.

It is good to see you, my friend.

As the light faded from her eyes, I recognized the soul within. She was the woman who raised Carmen's child for me, all those years ago. Somehow separated from the family line just for the purpose of creating my love.

The love I failed to protect.

My father answers and all the emotion inside me explodes. "They took my Forever Bound!" I shout, rage filling every inch of my being. "Thaddeus ripped her from our bed, he stole her and her family, killed her Babushka!"

I can hear the roars of my brothers in the background, the family raging with me. My father has gone dead quiet.

"You will not suffer her loss like I did when I lost your mother," he vows, his voice barely audible. "I will raze their homes to the ground, burn them all."

"Yes," I hiss.

My father chuckles. "It was the woman at your house, wasn't it?" But then his voice drops. "We'll get her back."

He hangs up and I turn to shadow, racing faster than I've ever moved before. My family will get there to save Kiera before I can, but I won't be far behind. The Monroes will pay for what they tried to take from me.

Mountains and valleys pass before me in a blur. I see nothing but my destination. I know nothing but that my mate, my love, is in danger.

It's nearly dawn before the Monroe castle comes into view, and it's circled by violence. Vampire fights vampire on the ground, winged vampires and shadow vampires ripping each other to shreds.

On a hill in the distance, I see my father battling with Thaddeus. Behind them Kiera is tied to a giant oak tree, battered and bloody. Two Monroe boys hold torches near her, piles of kindling around her feet, and Kiera is screaming.

I spear toward the battle, fury alive in my veins, landing on Thaddeus Monroe and joining the vicious fight. Together, my father and I attack; our shadows surrounding Thaddeus until he's in complete darkness. My claws rip ragged scars in his ugly face. Scars to match the one my mate left me, the first time she attacked because of his evil ways.

Yet each time I try, I can't get past him. He's more focused on keeping me here than killing me.

Because he knows the loss of Kiera will be far more painful.

Only a few yards away, Kiera slumps to her knees, still tied to the tree. A Monroe vampire shoots past us with a flaming torch and throws it on the tinder surrounding her.

"No!" I scream.

Thaddeus leaps onto me, digging his claws into my back. "Yes," he hisses.

His father rips him off me, only to be wrenched away by two Monroe sons. I turn away, the smell of smoke staining my lungs, desperate to get to my mate. A hand wraps around my throat, drawing me backward even as I flail, my heart shredding.

Kiera raises her head, her image now shimmering in the heat as the flames steadily grow, her gaze tortured. "I love you," she mouths.

"This is the end," Thaddeus sneers behind me.

"No, it's not," a woman yells.

My father and I freeze, the whole battlefield grows still as a Forever Bound mate to the Monroe clan walks onto the battlefield.

Black wings tipped with silver flare from her back, her white gown fluttering in the breeze as she floats towards us, her feet barely touching the ground. Her straight blonde hair floats behind her like a halo, and her blue eyes burn daggers into any man still battling. She lands on the ground, one massive beat of her wings extinguishing the fire.

Everyone on the battlefield has gone still, even Thaddeus.

"Angelica, you cannot be here... flee! Go! They will kill you!" he sputters, releasing me to run to her and fall at her feet, getting blood all over her gown as he clings to her desperately.

She looks down at him, furious, and kicks him away. "I'm done hiding while you waste precious lives for your foolish crusade! I will not watch you die! And I will not let you kill her!"

She points a sharp talon at Kiera, who's watching this just like everyone else, her skin pale beneath the ash and bruises.

I step towards her but get hit with a wing to the face, flying backwards to land on my backside.

"You don't take another step toward my mate or I'll kill you myself!" Angelica snarls. She grabs Thaddeus by his collar and drags him to the side, showing immense strength. With white talons, she slices the ropes tying Kiera to the tree and she catches her in her arms as she falls.

She turns, holding her almost tenderly, Thaddeus now forgotten. "Adam, she's weak. It is time."

She glares at her sons as they try to protest, and hisses at Thaddeus as he moves to fight her.

I run over, my mate near death in her arms, and black talons grow from my fingers. I want to kill them all, rip them limb from limb, but Angelica's hand grabs my face, her talons curling around the back of my head.

Her ice blue eyes bore into mine. "There is no time for revenge, your Forever Bound is dying. Will you seriously stand there and let a mother watch her daughter die?"

We never knew this woman existed, much less that she was this powerful, but the words she utters has me shocked to stillness. Angelica is Kiera's mother? She stares down at my Forever Bound, gently brushing hair from her face, and Kiera looks up at her in awe. The tears that fall from her eyes now are tears of sadness, of recognition. I knew that Kiera's mother had disappeared shortly after Emma was born. My background checks are very thorough.

I think back, twenty-five years ago, give or take, and realize that was a pivotal point in the war. Suddenly the Monroes became more vicious, more brutal. They were desperate, they had something to protect... Thaddeus had found his Forever Bound, Kiera's mother.

Angelica sits on the bloody ground, cradling Kiera in her arms. She whispers to her, and Kiera nods. Looking at them now, the resemblance is uncanny, but Angelica looks ethereal, like an angel descended to Earth to stop this battle. Kiera will mirror that strength soon, and she will outshine her mother with her beauty.

She holds Kiera's arm up to me. "Hurry, before it's too late once more."

I stop, shocked that she knows about the first time, but bite into Kiera's wrist even as I stare into the matriarch of the Monroe clan's eyes. Her mother's eyes...

Angelica strokes Kiera's hair, smiling down on her as I draw her blood into my body. I'm filled with heady euphoria even as I watch the color drain from Kiera's skin. Memories of the moment Anna died flood my mind, silencing any joy. Anna didn't survive. I was too late.

Or she never was my Forever Bound. And neither is Kiera.

Kiera smiles softly, lets out a sigh, and goes limp. Her head lolls to the side, her bloodless lips almost tilted in a smile. I'm frozen as I watch and wait.

As I yearn to see her eyes open, for her to lift her pale hand and touch me.

For my mate to return to me.

But nothing happens. Kiera doesn't move. Her body remains drained of life.

Her wrist drops from my mouth and I scream, roaring at the heavens as my heart shatters. The cruelest twist of hate couldn't have just repeated itself. I can't exist for eternity without her in it.

"Fool..." Angelica whispers. "Do you think this is an instantaneous thing? To become immortal and bear your children, Kiera has to die. Give me your hand!" She snatches it before I can move, putting it on Kiera's chest. "I feel it, do you?"

My back curves as shock robs me of strength. Kiera's skin is hardening, beginning to glow with new life. Her hair grows more vibrant, her wounds heal, leaving not even a trace of a scar except where I bit her on her wrist. Her body fills out, muscles expanding where she was soft and supple before. Finally, eyes like green fire fly open and she looks only at me.

Crying, I pull her from Angelica's arms. Kiera wraps her arms around my neck and I let out a strangled groan at the delicious feeling. She's so strong it feels like she's crushing me. Kiera can hurt me now, and she doesn't even realize she's squeezing too hard.

"I'm sorry! I'm so sorry! Can you forgive me? I love you so much. Let them kill me if I can't have you!" she sobs, clinging to me desperately.

Angelica's wings flap as she rises into the air. "Cadell's, I offer you this peace. Momentary peace! Take your woman and retreat. Leave now, take this mercy and go. I will not stop my mate a second time. Not even for my daughter..." Her eyes are soft and sad as she looks upon Kiera, but her fierce words echo in the night.

Every man hears them, as wings flap all around us and the Monroes leave together, following their powerful queen back to the castle. They'll no doubt watch, prepared to continue the battle if we do not accept this ceasefire, no matter how temporary it is.

For the first time since I lost Anna, the promise of peace beckons me.

I gaze down at her, emotions like wonder and awe filling me. "There's nothing to forgive, my love," I whisper.

In the distance, a black van screeches to a stop and Emma and Jenny are thrown out. Bruised, but alive. My brothers run to them, making sure they're okay as my father comes to stand over us. He's as bloody as I am, but otherwise unharmed.

"We will leave!" he roars, his arms in the air as he addresses our clan on the battlefield. "We have what we came for. My eldest son has his Forever Bound!" His voice drops, still equally as powerful as it carries over the bloody earth. "And we will return, stronger than ever."

The men cheer, and I kiss Kiera deeply. Tasting her. Reveling in her. Glorying in the truth that my future will be filled with this and so much more.

In that moment, I feel the change; her scent fluctuates as our fated bond takes hold. She's changed, her body metamorphosed to be able to support my seed, and in that moment we both know she's carrying the first child of the new generation.

I want to take her, right there on the bloody battlefield. "Go for twins?" I murmur.

Kiera smiles at me. She knows it too, I can smell she wants it as well. The helicopter lands nearby and I grab my moment. I sweep my love off her feet and take off running. I'm inside her on the floor of the helicopter before we even take off, heedless to what anyone may think. Kiera wraps her legs around my waist and her ankles lock.

I'm so surprised by her new and impressive strength that I stop, looking down at her in awe. She reaches down and strokes her stomach.

She knows. I know.

I thrust into her again, but slowly, tenderly. She carries the future inside her, and I will protect her from every enemy. Even if that means fucking her softly when all I want to do is rut like a wild animal until neither of us can move anymore.

Ready for the next installment in the Forever Bound series?
Check out Brec and Xanthe's story, Bound Blood!

BOUND BLOOD

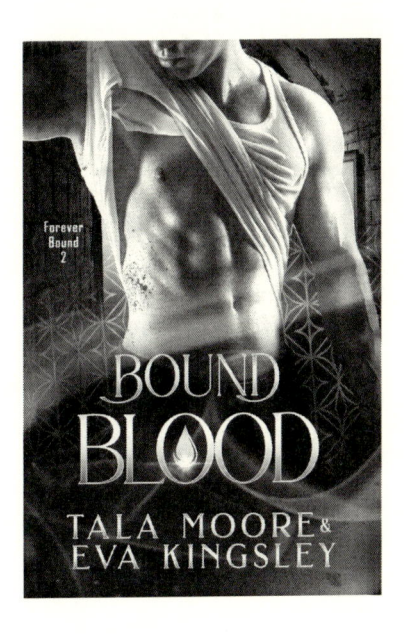

I refuse to be Forever Bound. I saw what the desperate search for the illusive mate of a vampire did to my father. And the women who died when he was wrong. I don't care what it means for the Cadell name or fortune.

To save an immortal life of lecturing, I need to find a stand in. A fake Forever Bound. And it turns out Xanthe is more than willing. She's fascinating, alive in ways I've never seen in my centuries-old existence, and fearless. Not even a grumpy vampire will stop her from getting what she wants.

Then I learn it's because Xanthe has nothing to lose.

Turns out, I could be the one who saves her. Or the one who kills her.

Brec and Xanthe are the perfect mix of grouchy and sunshine, and they're about to discover exactly how much they complete each other. Beck and Xanthe's story is a steamy, standalone romance with a HEA that will leave you smiling and sighing.

GRAB YOUR COPY HERE

https://mybook.to/BoundBlood

FREE READ!

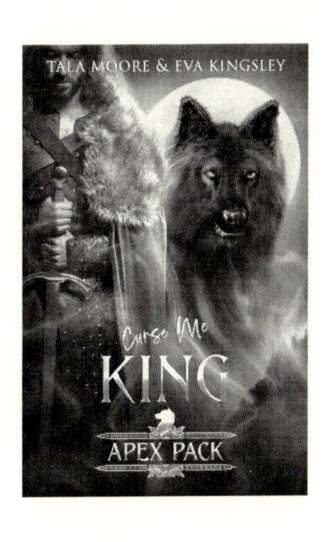

She cursed him as a punishment. It's a gift that changed everything.

He killed my friend, a goat I raised from birth, and for that, he shall pay. If the barbarian wants to act like a savage wolf, then he will live as one.

Except it's a King I've bound to my side. A furious one.

Nevertheless, Cassius is the enemy. He's rough and arrogant. Little did I know that underneath he's also honorable and protective.

His primal power is one I cannot deny.

Now we're trapped by a war I've always loathed, running for our lives, fighting growing feelings that neither of us understand.

Forces want Cassius' kingdom. But he now wants me, the witch who cursed him. I should say no. I want to say no.

FREE READ!

But I can't.

The spicy prequel to the Apex Pack Series. For fans of a strong heroine who's not afraid to wield her magic and the powerful King who will show her even that is no match for love. A steamy, standalone paranormal romance powerful enough to create the first werewolf.

FREE WHEN YOU SUBSCRIBE TO OUR NEWSLETTER!
https://dl.bookfunnel.com/xk2ljalgj8

Also by Tala Moore and Eva Kingsley

From the dynamic author duo who love fated mates!

APEX PACK

Find Me Tracker

Save Me Enemy

Mark Me Rogue

Match Me Wolf

Show Me How

Claim Me Alpha

Tie Me Down

Keep Me Safe

Catch Me Hunter

Heal Me Mate

Make Me Whole

TALA MOORE

SILVER MOON ALPHA

BLACK DIAMOND ALPHA

WILD HEART ALPHA

SHIFTER OBSESSION

EVA KINGSLEY

EMILY'S GAME

About the Authors

Tala Moore loves all things paranormal and romance. Give her possessive alpha males, sassy heroines, and a love that refuses to be denied, and she's set for as long as she can disappear from the world (which is never as long as she'd like!). Learn more about her books at on Amazon.

Eva Kingsley is a dark paranormal romance author who dives into your darkest desires and deepest fears. She's not afraid to describe the macabre and and still give a memorable and passionate (if not obsessive) love story. Connect with Eva on on Amazon.

Manufactured by Amazon.ca
Acheson, AB